A Shot in the Dark

A Shot in the Dark

Saki
(H.H. Munro)

ET REMOTISSIMA PROPE

Hesperus Classics

Hesperus Classics

Published by Hesperus Press Limited

4 Rickett Street, London SW6 1RU

www.hesperuspress.com

First published by Hesperus Press Limited, 2006

Introduction © Adam Newell, 2006

This selection © Hesperus Press, 2006

Foreword © Jeremy Dyson, 2006

Designed and typeset by Fraser Muggeridge studio

Printed in Jordan by Jordan National Press

ISBN: 1-84391-128-0

ISBN13: 978-1-84391-128-9

CONTENTS

FOREWORD

Saki. That single word nestling between the initialled surnames of his contemporaries on the contents page of *The Fourth Fontana Book of Ghost Stories*. Every other writer sounded so formal and stern – E.F. Benson, H.G. Wells, F. Marion Crawford. But here was one identified simply by a scant four letters. He seemed foreign, mischievous, like a character from Kipling – a talking mongoose or some such thing. I was nine years old and had become hooked on these anthologies. They must have been going cheap that year because I received three or four of them as birthday gifts from different sources. (I had, it seemed, acquired a reputation as a child who loved all things macabre and ghoulish.) Saki was a name that kept recurring from book to book – a constant presence whenever an editor set out to collect great stories of the supernatural. I knew nothing of literature, of why that might be the case. I just liked being scared.

But there was something peculiar about Saki's ghosts. They were never straightforward. The apparitions that so alarm the hapless visitor in 'The Open Window' turn out to be entirely flesh and blood, and the genuine air of menace evoked suddenly takes a satisfying swerve into the comic. The spirit of the oversized white hedgehog in 'The Hedgehog', which sounds funny (but as described, right down to its horribly clicking claws, is rather disturbing) is disingenuously explained away as being a painted prop pulled along on a bit of string. And then there were the ghost stories that didn't feature ghosts at all, but other, even more sinister forces. The prowling spirit of Pan in 'The Music on the Hill', or the worshipped ferret-god in 'Sredni Vashtar'. Even at nine years old I was able to detect a terrible wrongness in such pieces.

Revisiting Saki, many years later, I know a little more. That he was really an Englishman, like Kipling, born in the East. I know that he is revered as one of the greatest writers of short stories that ever lived – that he has remained in print constantly since his death ninety odd years ago. I know that the latter fact probably tells us more about the actual quality of an author's output than everything the critics have ever said about him. However, the lurking sense of mystery lingers. So it is a joy to have the opportunity to revisit Saki through a set of stories (and letters and sketches) that are completely unfamiliar, and see if, looked at in adulthood, they allow anything of that mystery to be unravelled.

There's an element of mischief in H.H. Munro's pseudonym (in reality he was as initialled as his contemporaries) that finds its echo in the stories themselves. His supernatural fiction often revels in locating a barely concealed brutality beneath the surface order of the Edwardian drawing room. His more overtly comic stories – much in evidence here – frequently do a similar thing. 'The East Wing' for example is quite merciless in its depiction of upper-middle class selfishness and stupidity, and other pieces such as 'The Almanack' and 'Tobermory' (with which Saki fans will already be familiar) also take pleasure in savaging that milieu. Viewed superficially his world of aunts, servants and long weekends in country houses might seem dated but his bright comic tone still reads fresh and modern. The aforementioned 'East Wing' features a marvellous piece of bathos whereby Canon Clore – who believes the inferno in the eponymous section of the house is an act of militant arson – makes a detailed 200-word defence of the suffragette cause only to be undercut by Major Boventry's wonderfully laconic response: 'Oughtn't we to be doing something about the fire'. (The joke's such a good one that Saki repeats it on the story's final page – and gets away with it.) Similarly contemporary in feel is the fragment of an unfinished story entitled 'The Garden of Eden' – a satirical take on Genesis 3. An unexpectedly righteous Eve is refusing to eat the forbidden fruit, despite the entreaties of the serpent, and an Archangel has been sent to speak to her, because she's messing up God's plans:

> '... No end of pictures of the Fall of Man are destined to be painted and a poet is going one day to write an immortal poem called Paradise L –'
>
> 'Called what?' asked Eve as the Archangel suddenly pulled himself up.
>
> 'Paradise Life. It's all about you and Adam eating the Forbidden Fruit. If you don't eat it I don't see how the poem can possibly be written.'

Saki's facility with character is unrivalled. Even in a lighter story such as 'The Pond' he succeeds instantly in creating a protagonist within a setting, which hooks you in by the end of the first paragraph. There's nothing flashy or grabby about his technique. It's subtle and refined but it works ruthlessly well. He often does two things at once, without you necessarily being aware he's doing either. In 'A Holy War' there is a comic exchange between Yealmton and his joyless wife Thirza that is ostensibly about the changes she has made to his beloved estate but is simultaneously a wonderful depiction of both their characters and a perceptive dialectic about materialism and less tangible values. The same story is a marvellous example of Saki's economy. It's terse and brief but it does an awful lot in a short space of time. It makes one think of Raymond Carver. Though on the surface the two writers could hardly be further apart, in fact they have a lot in common – the aforementioned skill with character and economy, together with an unexpected metaphysical air that hangs over seemingly ordinary events. Saki's best stories – as already observed – often make sudden but fulfilling last-minute changes of direction. In the case of 'A Holy War', from the comic to the diabolic; in 'The Pond', the route is opposite.

Another delightful aspect of Saki's work is his extraordinary nomenclature. An under-appreciated comic skill: it is the mark of our best comic writers that their characters' names alone make us laugh. In our own time Martin Amis, Chris Morris and Monty Python excel at this – Keith Talent, Collately Sisters and Mummy Badgerson are three favourites respectively. There are some marvellous examples in this collection. 'A Housing Problem' features two in the form of Mrs Duff-Chubleigh and Bobbie Chermbacon, whilst the title story features a reference to the county of Chalkshire. Like all the best comic names, for a brief moment you read it and think it's real.

Saki's work may also still feel fresh because of his apparent scepticism towards the prevailing values of his time (unlike Kipling). His supernatural fiction always suggested a certain cynicism about the British imperial project, evident in his fascination with the pagan and the repeated triumph of wild uncivilisable forces. The same can be said of a story like 'Tobermory' where a brute animal surgically eviscerates the supposed moral superiority of its masters – the wealthy upper classes. It is a story of which I'm particularly jealous. It is brilliantly comic and brilliantly bold and not many could pull it off in such a sparkling manner. Not only does the titular cat speak in clear English, but he is endowed with a superior cutting wit. And the reader buys it totally. It is pure pleasure.

Ultimately what makes Saki's fictions so vivid and vital a full century after they were written is the fact that their author was a speaker of truths. He saw clearly into the contradictions of the human heart and knew how to turn those tensions into entertainment. Consequently it's most likely these stories will remain alive and entertaining as long as there are human beings left to read them.

– Jeremy Dyson, 2006

It is a testament to Hector Hugh Munro's mastery of the short story that the collected works of Saki have never gone out of print. His invariably short, sharp tales leap effortlessly from weekends in the country to werewolves, from tea parties to talking cats, mixing satirical barbs at the mannered Edwardian society around him with the ever-present threat of an un-fettered, pagan wider world in which terrible things can, and usually do, happen. Tom Sharpe, one of the many distinguished authors (along with Noel Coward, Graham Greene, Will Self and now Jeremy Dyson) to have written an admiring foreword to a Saki collection, sums it up well: 'Step out through the French windows and you are in the realms of Pan…'

These days, the 140-odd collected Saki stories, two novels and three plays fit handily into one volume that, alas, is all too soon devoured. So, let us raise a glass of the driest champagne to celebrate this edition of rare and previously uncollected pieces, none of which are to be found amongst the pages of the so-called *Complete Saki*.

Munro originally wrote his stories for newspapers and magazines, such as *The Morning Post* and *The Bystander*, with his publishers (Methuen at first, and then The Bodley Head) issuing book-length collections every few years. Quite why the majority of the pieces presented here fell through the cracks, we shall probably never know. After his death in the First World War, Munro's sister Ethel compiled two posthumous collections, but one can only assume that Hector's records of what had been published where let her down.

What little we do know of Munro's life and character comes primarily from Ethel's brief biography of her brother. Originally included in the second posthumous book, *The Square Egg*, it has now been out of circulation for decades. While it is maddeningly selective ('I have not touched upon his social life, visits to country-house parties, etc.' she writes, 'as that would not be of interest'; generations of Saki readers would beg to differ), it does contain a few examples of Hector's writing unavailable elsewhere, two of which have been selected for this volume.

Hector was certainly no more forthcoming about himself. His only known interview, in an issue of The Bodley Head's publicity magazine *The Bodleian*, reveals only that, 'My favourite flower is the periwinkle; my favourite animal is the kingfisher, my favourite bird is the hedge sparrow, and I like oysters, asparagus and politics. Also the theatre.' A passage from his novel *When William Came* is perhaps more revealing, as one can be pretty certain that the description of the character Fritz von Kwarl also applies to his creator:

He was a bachelor of the type that is called confirmed and which might better be labelled consecrated; from his early youth onward to his present age he had never had the faintest flickering intention of marriage. Children and animals he adored, women and plants he accounted somewhat of a nuisance. A world without women and roses and asparagus would, he admitted, be robbed of much of its charm, but with all their charm these things were tiresome and thorny and capricious, always wanting to climb or creep in places where they were not wanted, and resolutely drooping and fading away when they were desired to flourish. Animals on the other hand, accepted the world as it was and made the best of it, and children, at least nice children, uncontaminated by grown-up influences, lived in worlds of their own making.

It is fitting then that 'Dogged', which is as far as we know Munro's first published short story, features an animal making the very best of the world it finds itself in, to the utter ruin of its owner. When the story originally appeared in *St Paul's* magazine on 18th February 1899, it was under the initials 'H.H.M.'; Munro did not use his famous pen name until the following year. Though the story is undeniably a little rough around the edges compared to later triumphs, its merits are more than enough to belatedly admit it into the official Saki canon.

'Travelling with Aunt Tom' is a letter from Hector to his sister, written from Edinburgh on 17th August 1901. A comic tour de force, it is one of the small selection of letters that Ethel deigned to include in her biography, before reportedly destroying her brother's remaining papers. With his mother dead and his father abroad, looming large in Hector's early life were the maiden aunts who brought him up, Augusta and Charlotte (who was always known as Tom). The thwarting of formidable aunts is of course a recurring theme in Saki – 'The Lumber-Room' is a particularly memorable example – though in this real-life situation, Hector is simply a passive, if increasingly exhausted, observer. The exquisitely annoying Aunt Tom later appeared, thinly disguised, in the story 'The Sex that Doesn't Shop'.

The world was introduced to Saki in 1900, with 'The Westminster Alice', a series of short satirical pieces in the *Westminster Gazette* that took Lewis Carroll's beloved character into the world of contemporary politics. It was a huge success, and Munro followed it in 1902 with a pastiche of a book published only months before. Calling his new series 'The Political Jungle Book', (and later the 'Not-So Stories') he continued to lampoon prominent politicians. The Prime

Minister Arthur Balfour, for example, became Sheer Khan't the tiger. ('When he went foraging his quarry was usually a scapegoat.'). The last and longest of the half a dozen Kipling-inspired sketches, 'A Jungle Story' was originally published in *The Morning Post* in late 1903. Its portrayal of authority's weary contempt for the political system stings just as much today as it did a century ago.

'The Garden of Eden' is an unfinished story found by Ethel and originally included in her biography. Hector has great fun introducing us to a stubbornly recalcitrant Eve, but we're left not knowing how she was finally persuaded to eat the apple. Perhaps Munro put the story aside when he simply couldn't think of a way.

'The Pond', and the five stories that follow it, were all discovered by A.J. Langguth when he was combing through magazine and newspaper archives for his definitive biography *Saki: A Life of Hector Hugh Munro*. Originally published in either *The Bystander* or *The Morning Post* between February 1912 and December 1913, they form a particularly rich little seam of neglected Saki, and are, as Langguth notes, 'more typical of his style than most of what appears in *The Square Egg*'. The pall of a malignant natural world is present and correct in both 'The Pond' and 'The Holy War', played for comic effect in the former but veering into tragedy in the latter. 'The Almanack' sees the welcome return of that 'mass of selfishness' Clovis Sangrail, and chronicles his entry into the predictions business. 'A Housing Problem' is another variation on one of Munro's favourite themes – a crisis at a house party – while 'A Sacrifice to Necessity', like 'The Stake' (a story that did make it into the collected works), warns against the perils of gambling. 'A Shot in the Dark' meanwhile takes another favourite theme, mistaken identity, and gives it a delicious twist.

'The East Wing' was originally published in the obscure American book *Lucas' Annual* in 1914, and has evaded Saki anthologists ever since. Subtitled 'A Tragedy in the Manner of the Discursive Dramatists', Munro is no doubt taking aim at one of his bugbears, George Bernard Shaw, and not for the first time: a few years after Shaw's *Man and Superman* was published, Munro cheekily entitled a collection *Beasts and Superbeasts*. 'The East Wing' is vintage Saki, and, considering its pivotal revelation that a beloved child is imaginary, it would be fascinating to know whether a more recent discursive dramatist, Edward Albee, ever read it.

Munro himself didn't have much success in the theatre. His only full-length play, a drawing-room comedy called *The Watched Pot*, went unproduced in his lifetime. Ethel nevertheless included it, and two earlier one-act pieces, in *The Square Egg* in 1924, but she left out a third Saki playlet, 'The Miracle Merchant'. Hector's adaptation of his Clovis story 'The Hen' eventually emerged a decade or so later in the eighth volume of a series called *One-Act Plays for Stage and Study*, never to be seen again until now. Though the action follows the original story fairly closely, Clovis has been replaced by the similarly louche Louis Courcet, and there is some additional stage business to up the tempo.

As is not surprising for the author of *When William Came*, the 1913 novel that foresaw a German-occupied England, Munro enlisted to fight in the First World War at the earliest opportunity. He wrote a breezily amusing insight into one aspect of his duties, 'On Being Company Orderly Corporal', while still stationed in England. Originally intended for his regiment's magazine, it also appeared in *The Bystander*, in June 1915. Munro was killed in action in France the following year.

To round off this collection is 'Tobermory', deservedly one of Saki's best-loved tales and perhaps his most memorable collision of genteel society and the supernatural. Presented here is the original version of the story, as it was printed in the *Westminster Gazette* on 27th November 1909. Munro later rewrote it, adding an appearance by the titular character of his next book collection, *The Chronicles of Clovis*. While the differences between the two versions are not great, frankly any excuse to enjoy this masterpiece should not be missed.

Why is Saki still so popular, and still striking a chord with readers in the 21st century? In the words of A.J. Langguth, whose meticulously researched biography is the best account of Munro's life we could ever hope to have, it is because society is finally catching up. In the years since he was writing, we have 'absorbed so many artistic and political shocks that Munro's ruthlessness and lack of sentimentality have made him modern and kept him fresh… Saki, aloof and condescending in his own time, turns out to be one of us.'

– Adam Newell, 2006

A Shot in the Dark

DOGGED

Artemus Gibbon was, by nature and inclination, blameless and respectable, and under happier circumstances the record of his life might have preserved the albino tint of its early promise; but he was of timid and yielding disposition, and had been carefully brought up, so that his case was clearly hopeless from the first. It only remained for the strong and unscrupulous character to come alongside, and the result was a foregone conclusion. And one afternoon it came. It is a well-tried axiom that, in human affairs, as in steeplechasing, the ugliest croppers occur at the 'safest' and most carefully pruned places, and of all conceivable occasions for a young man to go irretrievably wrong, a church bazaar would seem to offer the least appropriate opportunity. Yet it was at such a function, opened by a bishop's lady, and patronised by the most hopelessly correct people in the neighbourhood, that Artemus Gibbon went unsuspectingly to his undoing.

In the first place it must be admitted that his natural timidity was played upon by the embarrassing absence of anything at the bazaar that a bachelor of prosaic tastes might reasonably be expected to purchase with any approach to hearty conviction that his money was profitably laid out. Baby linen, which seemed to be the staple article on most of the stalls, was not to be thought of for a moment and the innate modesty of his taste in dress caused him to recoil from the 'Jubilee Memento Scarves', hand-worked with the royal arms in a delirium of crimson and gold. Hence, when he had purchased a harmless and unnecessary pincushion and two views of Durham Cathedral, he felt that he might, without odium, effect a dexterous retreat. Here it was that the Foreseen and Inevitable stepped in and changed the placid current of his life. He was pounced upon by a severe-looking dame, with an air of one being in authority, who gave him to understand that it was required of him that he should buy a dog.

'Only two guineas; my niece has charge of him over there. Clara!' Gibbon found himself a moment later confronted by a vivacious damsel – and the dog. The possibility of admitting a canine companion within the narrow compass of his establishment had not been altogether foreign to his speculations on life; a quiet, meek-eyed spaniel for instance, which would occupy an unobtrusive position by his domestic hearth, or participate in his constitutional walks, or, in later days, perhaps, a dignified deerhound with a tendency to statuesque repose – such were the shapes that his occasional ruminations on the subject had taken. But the dog now before him was by no means built according to these patterns. A rakish-looking fox terrier, stamped with the hallmark of naked and unashamed depravity, and wearing the yawningly alert air of one who has found the world is vain and likes it all the better for it, such was the specimen of dog-flesh at which Mr Artemus Gibbon found himself gazing in blank dismay.

Before he had quite realised the full force of the cataclysm in which he was involved, he had parted with the demanded forty-two shillings, and learned from the vivacious damsel the appalling fact that his new purchase was named Beelzebub. Something instinctively told him that he had parted too with his peace of mind, and as he was towed out of the bazaar premises in the wake of a yelping and plunging terrier, with an accompaniment of noise and publicity uncongenial to his natural modesty, he was dimly aware that he had started on a downgrade path that led to no good and peaceful end. To the ordinary intellect his position might not have appeared irretrievable; the dog that he had been rushed into buying, and whose personality inspired him with the strongest repugnance, was not necessarily a fixture. An immediate purchaser might be discovered, or the undesired acquisition might be given away, lost, or otherwise disposed of.

But here again the working of inexorable laws sterilised the chances of Gibbon's emancipation. In a conflict between their respective will powers, the man inevitably succumbed to the fox terrier, and, when the dinner-hour exposed the bachelor's sitting room to the observation of a tray-bearing handmaiden, its occupant was discovered in a condition of deprecatory embarrassment; whilst the dog, snugly ensconced in the only armchair, was the embodiment of self-composure and critical appraisement. As a general rule, Gibbon was not demonstratively communicative with maidservants, and his intercourse in this direction was usually limited to a perfunctory (vocal) salutation, or a mild request for a forgotten napkin, or such-like trifle. But the advent of Beelzebub had already dislocated the wonted disposition of affairs, and the girl became aware that an appeal of some nature was being addressed to her.

'Er, Mary, this little dog, er, I think you – might say nothing about it to Mrs Mulberry, er, just yet, that is, I will break it to her – I mean – will tell her myself – tomorrow morning.' While Gibbon was delivering himself of this charge he was shoving a warm, moist shilling Mary-wards along the table with a succession of short pats, as if he thought the coin should have some impetus of its own, and start forward in the desired direction. The hush money staved off the crisis that must assuredly arise when the landlady became aware of the canine presence in her apartments, and Gibbon, having successfully smuggled the contraband article into his bedroom, congratulated himself on having so far made the best of the situation. But, as the dog slipped out next morning on the incoming of the hot water, and chivvied the landlady's cat into the landlady's bedroom, and followed it onto her bed and under the blankets, where a muffled but vigorous battle royal ensued, it became doubtful whether the shilling had been, after all, a judicious outlay.

Gibbon found that his selection of new rooms was considerably narrowed by the prejudice aroused in the breasts of prospective landladies on the sight of his canine satellite, who accompanied him as a matter of course on all his quests; and finally, having strayed into a suite of chambers furnished in a style of bohemian extravagance that was wholly out of keeping with his accustomed ways of life, the terrier clinched matters for him by settling down therein and refusing to leave. Gibbon hunted him ineffectually round the place, upset and disarranged the furniture, all to no purpose; and at length, on the suggestion of the proprietor – 'you'd better take the rooms, sir, seems as if it was meant like' – he took alarm at the idea of resisting the possible workings of a Higher Power, and yielded. It was the weak character pitted against the strong once more, and the result was as it ever must be.

To the deteriorating effects of baneful companionship were now added the subtle workings of the laws of environment. Gibbon was too bashfully diffident to remove even the most glaringly uncongenial adornments of his new quarters, and it was a sign of his drifting progress that the views of Durham Cathedral did not find hanging room on the well-covered walls. Instead of these solidly respectable works of art, his eyes were daily confronted with presentiments of ladies who had apparently conquered the love of dress that is attributed to their sex, interspersed with portraits of racehorses noted for their fastness, or of society beauties with a similar reputation. But the chief agent in the moral slump that was becoming more and more pronounced in the person of Artemus Gibbon was undoubtedly Beelzebub. The very name was a stumbling block to the leading of a respectable life, and a young man who called an already sufficiently unprepossessing animal by such an unseemly appellation was doomed to be dropped by self-respecting acquaintants.

Then with change of friends came also change of habits. Sober constitutionals became a thing of the past since Beelzebub, speedily bored by such tame affairs, contracted a habit of jumping into the nearest empty hansom; the cabman naturally pulled up, and as the dog would not get out, Gibbon had to get in. Having no address that he could give at the moment – it usually happened a few yards from his own door – a restaurant became the necessary destination, and Beelzebub never left much before closing-time. The eye of the waiter, scornfully regarding his slowly emptied glass of lager, invariably impelled the naturally temperate Gibbon to order another drink, and the homeward cab was sometimes a matter of convenience as well as dictation.

As fast as the fate-driven dissipator alienated old acquaintances, Beelzebub supplied him with new ones of a stamp more congruous with his altered circumstances; smart sporting youths, lurid in waistcoats and conversation, foregathered with the guileless owner of the indiscriminately social terrier, and one by one the landmarks of the placid past were swept away. Awaking in the harsh crude light of mature morning from late and unrefreshing sleep, Artemus would cast his eyes wearily round his disordered rooms, and everywhere the trail of the dog met his gaze, in powdery cigarette ashes, empty liqueur glasses, vivid-hued sporting periodicals, and tumbled packs of cards.

But the finishing touch was yet to come. Sitting one night in a café where he and his dog were now recognised habitués, slowly imbibing the Scotch and soda that had supplanted the lager of his earlier dissipations, Gibbon had momentarily lost himself in that superstructure of woe that consists of 'remembering be happier things'; in particular he was thinking of a certain prodigally inclined young friend of his pre-canine days, by name Hilary Helforlether, whom he had tried to keep, by the force of example and precept, in the straight and narrow way that leads to a respected old age. From the uncomfortable reflections to which this reverie gave rise, he was suddenly aroused by a screamlet of vexed consternation, and turning sharply beheld at an adjoining table a lady, whose entrance had languidly attracted his attention some quarter of an hour ago. She was young and pretty and birdlike – especially with regard to her hair, which was of the tint a Norwich Canary aspires to but seldom attains – and there was just a delicate flavour of a possible foreign extraction about her; her attire was a rhapsody (with lucid intervals) of purple and gold, and a magnificent boa of ostrich feather had supplied the finishing touch to an impressive costume. The soft shimmering lengths of this elegant accessory had attracted the attention of the ever-alert Beelzebub, who had quietly abstracted it as it hung negligently from its owner's chair, and by a process of 'little and often' had conscientiously given to each individual feather a separate and independent existence.

Gibbon's horrified gaze, attracted by the lady's excusable agitation, rested on his graceless quadruped snoozing amid the ruin of fluffiness like an eider-duckling in its nest. 'No marvel that the lady wept', or would have if consideration for her complexion had not prevailed, and Beelzebub's owner hastened to gasp out a little hurricane of apologies and enquiries as to the estimated cost of the damage.

The lady really behaved very sweetly considering her provocation, and if in her agitation she placed the price of her ravaged boa somewhat above its Bond Street level, it was only in accordance with the impulse that teaches us to value things the more when we have lost them. Gibbon had not the amount on him, would the lady give him her address, or, well, yes, perhaps that would be better, he would give her his card, tomorrow afternoon, unfailingly, etc., etc., and before he knew what he was doing he had made an assignation with the boa-bereaved damsel.

Gibbon had never before given tea to a lady in his apartments, and was necessarily rather inept in his administration of this unwonted hospitality, but his fair guest supplied the deficiencies of his experience, and knew exactly when the milder beverage should be followed up by liqueurs and cigarettes. That she was not dissatisfied with her entertainment her host gathered from the fact that she graciously forestalled his invitation to come again and continue his education in the art of tea-giving. In short, she was altogether in affable mood, and if she forgot to give the overwhelmed Gibbon any change for his tenner, she at least atoned for the omission by favouring him with a wholly spontaneous kiss.

This unsolicited kindness was conferred on him while opening his outer door for his visitor's departure, which was the appropriate psychological moment for its delivery; it was unfortunate, nevertheless, that Hilary Helforlether should have chosen the same moment for appearing hull-down on the staircase horizon. Artemus, having sped the parting guest, greeted his new visitor with a hastily mobilised smile that suffered by comparison with the grin on his sometime disciple's face.

'Oh, you pipeclayed sepulchre! Thought you were the blamed whiting of a lifeless flower, and all that sort of thing. *Rats!* Hullo, what a jolly terrier. Does he belong to you?'

'No; I belong to him. Body and soul,' muttered Gibbon, drearily.

TRAVELLING WITH AUNT TOM

My Dear E.

Travelling with Aunt Tom is more exciting than motorcarring. We had four changes and on each occasion she expected the railway company to bring our trunks round on a tray to show that they really had them on the train. Every ten minutes or so she was prophetically certain that her trunk, containing among other things 'poor mother's lace', would never arrive at Edinburgh. There are times when I almost wish Aunt Tom had never had a mother. Nothing but a merciful sense of humour brought me through that intermittent unstayable outpour of bemoaning. And at Edinburgh, sure enough her trunk was missing!

It was in vain that the guard assured her that it would come on in the next train, half an hour later; she denounced the vile populace of Bristol and Crewe, who had broken open her box and were even then wearing the maternal lace. I said no one wore lace at eight o'clock in the morning and persuaded her to get some breakfast in the refreshment room while we waited for the alleged train. Then a worse thing befell – no baps! There were lovely French rolls but she demanded of the terrified waiter if he thought we had come to Edinburgh to eat bread!

In the midst of our bapless breakfast I went out and lit upon her trunk and got a wee bit laddie to carry it in and lay it at her very feet. Aunt Tom received it with faint interest and complained of the absence of baps.

Then we spent a happy hour driving from one hostelry to another in search of rooms, Aunt Tom reiterating the existence of a Writer to the Signet[1] who went away and let his rooms thirty years ago, and ought to be doing it still. 'Anyhow,' she said, 'we are seeing Edinburgh,' much as Moses might have informed the companions of his forty years' wanderings that they were seeing Asia. Then we came here, and she took rooms after scolding the manageress, servants and entire establishment nearly out of their senses because everything was not to her liking. I hurriedly explained to everybody that my aunt was tired and upset after a long journey, and disappointed at not getting the rooms she had expected; after I had comforted two chambermaids and the boots, who were crying quietly in corners, and coaxed the hotel kitten out of the waste-paper basket, I went to get a shave and a wash – when I came back Aunt Tom was beaming on the whole establishment and saying she should recommend the hotel to all her friends. 'You can easily manage these people,' she remarked at lunch, 'if you only know the way to their hearts.' She told the manageress that I was frightfully particular. I believe we are to be here till Tuesday morning, and then go into rooms; the hotel people have earnestly recommended a lot to us.

Aunt Tom really is marvellous; after sixteen hours in the train without a wink of sleep, and an hour spent in hunting for rooms, her only desire is to go out and see the shops. She says it was a remarkably comfortable journey; personally I have never known such an exhausting experience.

Y.a.b.

[your affectionate brother]

H.H. Munro

Mowgli the bare-limbed and immortal opened his eyes expectantly and spoke to the Other:

'I have told you of the Jungle and its laws. Tell me of the tangle that you call your political system.'

'Pardon me,' said the Other, 'I never called it a system. Though perhaps,' he added, 'it has fixed laws of an unobtrusive character.'

'But you must have a ruling Caste?'

'We are beginning to recognise the necessity, and one day no doubt we shall invent one. At present we are being looked after by a great course of politicians, some of whom will become statesmen in the course of time, if they don't take up some useful employment in the meanwhile.'

'Tell me,' said Mowgli, 'how they grow into statesmen.'

'First, when they are about eighteen or twenty they read about Pitt and Burke and Talleyrand[2] and other real people; that is their hopeful, enquiring stage, and it is often their best. Then most of them go into the Parrot House of party politics and hear nothing but parrot cries from one year to another.'

'What are the parrot cries?'

'Oh, they are too many to remember. "Unearned increment", "Standard of living", "Peace at any price", "Union of hearts", "Trade follows the flag", "Fight to a finish", "Back to the land", "Food of the people", "Efficiency with economy" – that is the language in which the Parrot House thinks, and any time that you like to leave your wolf-pack and come and listen you will find it thinking that way still; the Parrot House always thinks aloud.'

Mowgli yawned. 'Now tell me about the statesmen,' he said. The Other considered.

'The least troublesome way of becoming a statesman is to marry, only of course you must marry the right people. The laws of this country only permit one wife at a time to each man, so you see it isn't so simple as it sounds to become a statesman by marriage. Then an amiable, genial personality counts for a great deal; a drop of honey catches more flies, etc., which is an excellent counsel as long as you limit yourself to flies. Certainly there are men who force themselves to the front by strength of character and ability, but we are never quite sure whether we like that kind of statesman; as a rule it is inclined to be brusque and to say things which in our thinking moments we suspect to be true.'

'But,' said Mowgli, 'the fittest must find his place when the need calls. So it is with us and it cannot be otherwise.'

'With us,' said the Other, 'it can. For example, as far as can be known there is only one statesman in England with a talent for foreign affairs, and we keep him in India. No, that isn't a paradox, it's a habit. It means putting your trust in improvidence.'

Mowgli considered deeply. 'And if any one of the men you have to depend on is lacking in grip or skill?' he asked.

'It is one of the laws of our tangle that a man is assumed to be competent till he has proved himself to be otherwise. And then –'

'And then,' broke in Mowgli, 'in the wolf-pack he would be torn to pieces.'

The Other gave him a grim chuckle. 'We are more cruel. We let the department go to pieces.'

'But if your headmen don't take greater care than that in what they have to do how is it you keep them at the Council Rock? Have you no others?'

'We have, and that is just the reason. When there are murmurs for a change the Government whistles up the leaders of the Opposition and shows them to the people. That is usually all that has to be done. Listen, Mowgli, and I will show you how things lie with us. Follow me in your mind's eye, taking Vladivostok, "the dominion of the East", as a starting point, down from the Manchurian country, along the great rivers that empty themselves into the Yellow Sea, up into the highlands of Tibet, across the Indus and on to the Afghan Plateau, away over to the Persian Gulf, and along the Tigris to Baghdad. Yes, and through Turkey into the wild Balkan Mountains, and back with a sweep to the Red Sea coast and the rolling African wastes that lie beyond it. That is our jungle, where we must hunt and be hunted, and that is only a part of it. And as the world grows smaller and the empires grow bigger the hunting will become keener and hotter, and they will sleep best who sleep least. That is the law in your jungle, and it is the same in ours.

'And now follow me into our homeland and see how we grasp and weigh the lie of things. Every now and again the folk of some township or district hold a choosing; not one-tenth of them could give you a guess at the different races inhabiting Asia and where each fitted in. It is an unwritten book to them. But they are busy putting little crosses against the names of the candidates, and when those little crosses are counted that is the supreme thing in all our political purpose. The politicians scan the totals breathlessly, and you hear them say one to another: "Compared with '92 we have increased by more than four hundred, and they have polled two hundred and fifty less." That is the thing that matters.'

'And you call that a political system?' said Mowgli.

'If you remember,' said the Other, 'I didn't.'

Mowgli the bare-limbed and immortal rose and stretched himself. 'I think,' he said, 'I will go back to the grey wolves.'

The Serpent elaborated all the arguments and inducements that he had already brought forward, and improvised some new ones, but Eve's reply was unfailingly the same. Her mind was made up. The Serpent gave a final petulant wriggle of its coils and slid out of the landscape with an unmistakable air of displeasure.

'You haven't tasted the Forbidden Fruit, I suppose?' said a pleasant but rather anxious voice at Eve's shoulder a few minutes later. It was one of the Archangels who was speaking.

'No,' said Eve placidly, 'Adam and I went into the matter very thoroughly last night and we came to the conclusion that we should be rather ill-advised in eating the fruit of that tree; after all, there are heaps of other trees and vegetables for us to feed on.'

'Of course it does great credit to your sense of obedience,' said the Archangel, with an entire lack of enthusiasm in his voice, 'but it will cause considerable disappointment in some quarters. There was an idea going about that you might be persuaded by specious arguments into tasting the Forbidden Fruit.'

'There *was* a Serpent here speaking about it the last few days,' said Eve; 'he seemed rather huffed that we didn't follow his advice, but Adam and I went into the whole matter last night and we came to t –'

'Yes, yes,' said the Archangel in an embarrassed voice, 'a very praiseworthy decision, of course. At the same time, well, it's not exactly what everyone anticipated. You see Sin has got to come into the world, somehow.'

'Yes ?' said Eve, without any marked show of interest.

'And you are practically the only people who *can* introduce it.'

'I don't know anything about that,' said Eve placidly; 'Adam and I have got to think of our own interests. We went very thoroughly –'

'You see,' said the Archangel, 'the most elaborate arrangements have been foreordained on the assumption that you *would* yield to temptation. No end of pictures of the Fall of Man are destined to be painted and a poet is going one day to write an immortal poem called Paradise L –'

'Called what ?' asked Eve as the Archangel suddenly pulled himself up.

'Paradise Life. It's all about you and Adam eating the Forbidden Fruit. If you don't eat it I don't see how the poem can possibly be written.'

Eve is still dogged – says she has no appetite for more fruit.

'I had some figs and plantains and half a dozen medlars early this morning, and mulberries and a few mangosteens in the middle of today, and last night Adam and I feasted to repletion on young asparagus and parsley-tops with a sauce of pomegranate juice; and yesterday morning –'

'I must be going,' said the Archangel, adding rather sulkily, 'if I should see the Serpent would it be any use telling him to look round again – ?'

'Not in the least,' said Eve. Her mind was made up.

'The trouble is,' said the Archangel as he folded his wings in a serener atmosphere and recounted his Eden experiences, 'there is too great a profusion of fruit in that garden; there isn't enough temptation to hunger after one special kind. Now if there was a partial crop failure...' The idea was acted on. Blight, mildew and caterpillars and untimely frosts worked havoc among trees and bushes and herbs; the plantains withered, the asparagus never sprouted, the pineapples never ripened, radishes were worm-eaten before they were big enough to pick. The Tree of Knowledge alone flaunted itself in undiminished luxuriance.

'We shall have to eat it after all,' said Adam, who had breakfasted sparsely on some mouldy tamarinds and the rind of yesterday's melon.

'We were told not to, and we're not going to,' said Eve stubbornly. Her mind was made up on the point…

THE POND

Mona had always regarded herself as cast for the tragic role; her name, her large dark eyes, and the style of hairdressing that best suited her all contributed to support that outlook on life. She habitually wore the air of one who has seen trouble, or, at any rate, expects to do so very shortly; and she was accustomed to speak of the Angel of Death almost as other people would speak of their chauffeur waiting around the corner to fetch them at the appointed moment. Fortune-tellers, noting this tendency in her disposition, invariably hinted at something in her fate that they would not care to speak about too explicitly. 'You will marry the man of your choice, but afterwards you will pass through strange fires,' a Bond Street two-guinea palm-oilist had told her. 'Thank you,' said Mona, 'for your plain speaking. But I have known it always.'

In marrying John Waddacombe, Mona had mated herself with a man who shared none of her intimacy with the shadowy tragedies of what she called the half-seen world. He had the substantial tragedies of his own world to bother about, without straining his eyes for the elusive and dubious distractions belonging to a sphere that lay entirely beyond his range of vision; or, for the matter of that, his range of interests. Potato blight, swine fever, the Government's land legislation, and other pests of the farm absorbed his attention as well as his energies, and even if he had admitted the possibility of such a disease as soul-sickness, of which Mona recognised eleven distinct varieties, most of them incurable, he would probably have prescribed a fortnight at the seaside as the most hopeful and natural remedy. There was no disguising the fact, John Waddacombe was of the loam, loamy. If he had cared to go into politics he would have been known inevitably as honest

John Waddacombe, and after that there is nothing more to be said.

Two days, or thereabouts, after her marriage, Mona had made the tragic discovery that she was yoked to a life-partner with whom she had little in common, and from whom she could expect nothing in the way of sympathetic understanding. Anyone else, knowing both her and John and their respective temperaments, could her have advanced her that information the moment that the engagement was announced. John was fond of her in his own way, and she, in her quite different way, was more than a little fond of him; but they trafficked in ideas that had scarcely a common language.

Mona set out on her married life with the expectation of being misunderstood, and after a while John arrived at the rather obvious conclusion that he didn't understand her – and was content to 'leave it at that'. His wife was at first irritated and then disheartened by his attitude of stolid indifference. 'Least said, soonest mended,' was his comfortable doctrine, which failed woefully when applied to Mona's share of the reticence. She was unhappy and perturbed about their lack of soul-fellowship; why couldn't he be decently distressed about it also? From being at first theatrically miserable she became more seriously affected. The morbid strain in her character found at last something tangible to feed on, and brought a good appetite to the feeding. While John was busy and moderately happy with his farm troubles, Mona was dull, unoccupied, and immoderately unhappy with her own trouble.

It was at this time, in the course of one of her moody, listless rambles, that she came across the pond. In the high chalky soil of the neighbourhood, standing water was a rarity; with the exception of the artificially made duck pond at the farm and one or two cattle pools, Mona knew of no other for miles around. It stood in a clay 'pocket' in the heart of a neglected beech plantation on the steep side of a hill, a dark, evil-looking patch of water, fenced round and overspread with gloomy yews and monstrous decaying beeches. It was not a cheerful spot, and such picturesqueness as it possessed was all on the side of melancholy; the only human suggestion that could arise in connection with the pool was the idea of a dead body floating on its surface. Mona took to the place with an instant-aneous sense of fascination; it suited her temperament, and it mightily suited her mood. Nearly all her walks led her to the beech wood, and the Mecca of the wood was always the still, dark pond, with its suggestion of illimitable depths, its silence, its air of an almost malignant despondency. If one could indulge in such a flight of fancy as to imagine a hill rejoicing, or a valley smiling, one could certainly picture the pond wearing a sullen, evil scowl.

Mona wove all sorts of histories about the pool, and in most of them there was some unhappy, fate-buffeted soul who hung wearily over its beckoning depths and finally floated in sombre spectacular repose among the weeds on its surface, and each time that she reshaped the story she identified the victim more and more with herself. She would stand or sit on the steeply inclined bank that overhung the pond on every side, peering down into the water and reflecting on the consequences that would follow a slip of her foot or an incautious venturing over-near the edge. How long would she struggle in those unfathomed weed-grown depths before she lay as pictur-esquely still as the drowned heroine of her tale-weavings, and how long would she float there in peace, with the daylight and moonlight reaching down to her through the overarching catafalque of yew and beech, before searchers discovered her resting-place, and hauled her body away to the sordid necessities of inquest and burial? The idea of ending her despondencies and soul troubles in that dark, repose-inviting pool took firmer and clearer shape; there seemed a spirit lurking in its depths and smiling on its surface that beckoned her to lean further and yet further over its edge, to stand more and more rashly on the steep slope that overhung it. She took a subtle pleasure in marking how the fascination grew on her with each visit; how the dread of the catastrophe that she was courting grew less and less. Every time that she reluctantly tore herself away from the spot there seemed a half-jeering, half-reproachful murmur in the air around her, 'Why not today?'

And then, at a timely moment, John Waddacombe, hearty as an ox, and seemingly proof against weather exposure, fell suddenly and critically ill with a lung attack that nearly triumphed over doctors and nurses and his own powers of stubborn resistance. Mona did her fair share of the nursing while the case was critical, fighting with greater zeal against the death that threatened her husband than she had shown in combating the suggestion of self-destruction that had gained so insidious a hold on her. And when the convalescent stage had been reached she found John, weak and rather fretful as he was after his long experience of the sick-room, far more lovable and sympathetic than he had been in the days of his vigour. The barriers of reserve and mutual impatience had been broken down, and husband and wife found that they had more in common than they had once thought possible. Mona forgot the pond, or thought of it only with a shudder; a healthy contempt for her morbid weakness and silliness had begun to assert itself. John was not the only one of them who was going through a period of convalescence.

The self-pity and the coquetry with self-destruction had passed away under the stress of new sympathies and interests; the morbid undercurrent was part of Mona's nature, and was not to cast out at a moment's notice. It was the prompting of this undercurrent that led her, one day in the autumn, to pay a visit to the spot where she had toyed so weakly with stupid, evil ideas and temptations. It would be, she felt, a curious sensation to renew acquaintance with the place now that its fascination and potential tragedy had been destroyed. In outward setting it was more desolate and gloom-shrouded than ever; the trees had lost their early autumnal magnificence, and rain had soaked the fallen beech leaves into a paste of dark slush under foot. Amid the nakedness of their neighbours, the yews stood out thick, and black, and forbidding, and the sickly growth of fungoid things showed itself prominently amid the rotting vegetation. Mona peered down at the dark, ugly pool, and shuddered to think that she could ever have contemplated an end so horrible as choking and gasping to death in those foul, stagnant depths, with their floating surface of slime and creeping water insects and rank weed-growth. And then the thing that she recoiled from in disgust seemed to rise up towards her as though to drag her down in a long-deferred embrace. Her feet had slipped on the slithery surface of sodden leaves and greasy clay, and she was sliding helplessly down the steep bank to where it dropped sheer into the pool. She clutched and clawed frantically at yielding roots and wet, slippery earth, and felt the weight of her body pull her downward with ever-increasing momentum. The hideous pool, whose fascination she had courted and slighted, was gaping in readiness for her; even if she had been a swimmer there would have been little chance for her in those weed-tangled depths, and John would find her there, as once she had almost wished – John who had loved her and learned to love her better than ever; John whom she loved with all her heart. She raised her voice to call his name again and again, but she knew he was a mile or two away, busy with the farm life that once more claimed his devoted attention. She felt the bank slide away from her in a dark, ugly smear, and heard the small stones and twigs that she had dislodged fall with soft splashes into the water at her feet; above her, far above her it seemed, the yews spread their sombre branches like the roof-span of a crypt.

'Heavens alive, Mona, where did you get all that mud?' asked John in some pardonable astonishment. 'Have you been playing catch-as-catch-can with the pigs? You're splashed up to the eyes in it.'

'I slipped into a pond,' said Mona.

'What, into the horse pond?' asked John.

'No, a pond out in one of the woods,' she explained.

'I didn't know there was such a thing for miles around,' said John.

'Well, perhaps it would be an exaggeration to call it a pond,' said Mona with a faint trace of resentment in her voice; 'it's only about an inch and a half deep.'

THE HOLY WAR

Revil Yealmton sat in the swaying dining car of a Nord Express train that raced westward through the Prussian plain in the dusk of an early summer day. After nearly two years of profitable business pilgrimage in the border regions of Asiatic Russia he was returning to wife and home in the English West Country. It was a house that, as a matter of fact, he had never inhabited, and yet he was looking forward to reaching it as eagerly as though it had been the hallowed dwelling place of his childhood. Old memories endeared the place to his recollection, even though they were the memories of one who had dreamed rather than of one who had experienced. In his early days, when he had lived with his parents in a prim and rather dreary cottage in a sleepy West Country village, the old gabled house at the foot of the hill had been occupied by a bachelor uncle, who had not encouraged his relatives to intrude too freely on his seclusion. From the evergreen fastness of a conveniently placed holly hedge the boy had been able to look, unobserved, on the domain with which he seldom enjoyed closer acquaintance, and in his eyes it had been a wonderful and desirable abode for mortal man. Every detail stood up in his mind now with undimmed distinctness as he sat finishing his dinner in the jolting train. There was the broad pond at the entrance, whereupon a company of drakes and ducks, mottled and ring-straked and burnished, went to and fro like a flotilla of painted merchantmen on an inland sea; there were high white gates that led into a yew-begirt garden on one side and a wide straw-yard on the other, a yard in which radiant-plumaged gamecocks led their attendant trains of hen folk in endless busy forays, and sleek, damson-hued pigs grubbed and munched and dozed the day long. And on the hillside beyond the yard there was an orchard of unspeakable delight, where the goldfinches nested in the spring, and the apples and greengages and cherries made one's eyes ache with longing in fruit time. There were a hundred other heart-enslaving things that he remembered from his boyhood's days, and the wonder was that the clamour of them had stood the critical test of maturing years. After his parents had passed into a pious memory he had revisited the neighbourhood with the assurance of a successful mercantile career to his credit, and had found the old uncle more humane and friendly than of yore, and the old gabled house and all that stood with it as bewitching as ever. And then, a few months later, as he had been setting out on his important eastward journey, the uncle had died and left his nephew all that earthly paradise to have and to hold. Yealmton had sent his wife to take possession, and deferred the joy of entering into his desired land until he should have seen his Russian enterprise to a successful conclusion. And now he was returning, with a riot of expectant longing in his brain, to his home – and to Thirza. But a thought kept intruding itself with unwelcome cynicism: was his wife really included in the anticipations that piled themselves so pleasantly before him?

Thirza Yealmton was what is known as a managing woman. Of such there are many that are only to be spoken of with honour and incense-burning, but Thirza was of the regrettable kind that can never realise that nature, and particularly human nature, is sometimes devised and constructed to be unmanageable, for its own happiness and its own good. Yealmton thought, with a suppressed psalm of thanksgiving at the back of his mind, of the comfortable discomfort of his last two years of travel, and of how Thirza's presence on the scene would assuredly have entailed a distressing accompaniment of arranging and supervising and general dislocation of the accepted way of things. He knew that he was impatiently counting the slow hours that separated him from the old homestead at the foot of the hill, but he could not reassure himself that any of the impatience was honestly due to a desire to be once more in his wife's company and within the sphere of her organising genius.

Later, when Thirza met him with the pony-cart at the small country station, Yealmton knew that his cynical self-accusation had been well founded. The anticipation still ran high in his brain and heart; none of it had found realisation in the meeting with his wife. It was unfortunate, he admitted to himself, but he was too engrossed with other crowding sensations to give the matter more than a perfunctory vote of censure. He hardly heeded Thirza's unstemmed torrent of talk that kept pace with the rattle of pony's hoofs, until a sentence detached itself with unpleasant distinctness.

'You will find a lot of improvements since you last saw the place.'

'Improvements?'

He jerked out the question wonderingly. It had never crossed his mind that any improvement could be desirable in the wonderland that he remembered.

'For one thing,' said Thirza, as the cart swung round a corner and brought them into view of the gates, 'I've had that old pond at the entrance drained away; it made things damp and looked untidy.'

Yealmton said nothing, and Thirza did not see the look that came into his eyes. He remained silent, too, when his wife introduced him to a monotonous colony of white Leghorns, in wired runs, that she had substituted for the lively poultry yard of strutting, gorgon-hued game fowl that had been his uncle's special pride.

'The miller bought most of the old stock,' she informed him: 'a quarrelsome straying lot those game fowl were. I was glad to get rid of them. These ones are record layers, and I make quite a lot by their eggs. This is where the orchard was.'

She showed him a trim array of young fruit trees, planted in serried rows, in a carefully wooded enclosure.

'When they are fully grown they will yield three times the profit that the old orchard did,' she observed.

'We are not poor,' said Yealmton.

Thirza was chilled and offended; how little her husband appreciated the trouble she had been to in the matter.

'Money is always worth having,' she said sharply.

'Goldfinches used to build in the old orchard,' said Yealmton, almost to himself.

'Birds are a mistake about a garden, I think,' said Thirza: 'we could have goldfinches in an aviary if you liked.'

'I would not like,' said Yealmton, shortly.

A yellow figure came down a garden path and made straight for the newcomer.

'Hullo, Peterkin,' cried Yealmton, gladly, and a golden-furred cat sprang purring into his arms.

'How funny!' said Thirza. 'That cat hasn't been seen anywhere about the place since the first week I was here; I didn't know it was still in existence. Don't let it come into the house,' she added; 'I don't encourage cats about a house.'

For answer Yealmton carried Peterkin into the morning room and placed him on a broad shelf built into the inglenook.

'That was his throne in my uncle's time,' he said: 'It is his throne now.'

Thirza promptly decided on a four days' headache, which was her invariable recipe whenever anyone thwarted or annoyed her. She had been known to postpone it in times of stress, such as Christmas week or a spring cleaning, but she would never forgo it altogether. For the moment she said nothing.

After dinner that evening Yealmton stood at an open window, with Peterkin purring rapturously at his side, and listened for some remembered sound that should have come to him through the dusk.

'Why aren't the wood owls hooting?' he asked. 'They always used to call from the copse about this time. All the way across Europe I've been longing to hear those owls singing vespers.'

'Do you like their noise?' asked Thirza. 'I couldn't stand it. I got the local gamekeeper to shoot them. It was such a dismal noise, I think.'

'Is there any other vile thing that you have done in this dear old place?' asked Yealmton. He spoke to himself, but he asked the question aloud. Then he added: 'Something dreadful must surely happen to you!'

Thirza gasped and stared at him for half a minute.

'You are over-tired with your journey,' she said at last, and went upstairs to inaugurate a headache, which, she felt, could scarcely last less than a week.

Judicious digging operations restored the pond to something like its old splendour, and a great company of ducks, mottled and ring-straked and speckled, went to and fro on its waters as though they had been doing it all their lives. A couple of young gamecocks, supplied by the sympathetic miller, made short work of the alien white cockerels that had reigned in their stead, and the local gamekeeper was warned of the dismal things that would befall him if any further owl slaughter was brought home to his account. Even the fruit paddock was induced to lose some of its nursery-garden air and to stray back toward the glory of a West Country orchard. The birds of heaven received no further discouragement, except such as was meted out to them by Peterkin in his capacity of warden of the currant bushes. And while these things were being done Yealmton and his wife waged a politely reticent warfare; it was a struggle that Thirza knew she must ultimately win, because she was fighting for existence – arranging and interfering and supervising were a necessary condition of her well-being. What she did not know, or did not understand, was that Yealmton was fighting a Holy War, and therefore could not be defeated.

As summer and autumn passed away into winter Thirza turned her managing energies in a greater degree upon the rural life of the village, where she encountered less formidable obstacles than Yealmton's overruling opposition presented in the narrower sphere. She was not popular with the cottagers, but she had thoroughly mastered the art of being penetrating.

'I am going down to the millponds,' she announced one afternoon, when a hard frost had held the land for a couple of days; 'the children will be coming out of school about now. They've been warned not to go on the ice, and I mean to see that they don't.'

'It can't possibly bear yet,' said Yealmton.

'It bears at the shallow end,' said Thirza.

'Then why not let them go on the shallow end?' asked Yealmton.

'They've been told not to,' said Thirza; 'I don't wish to argue the matter. I mean to see that none of them go on.'

As a matter of fact the children were engrossed with a slide at the other end of the village, and Thirza had the lonely mill meadows to herself. From the orchard gate Yealmton could see her walking rapidly along the reed-fringed borders of the wide ponds, as though determined to see no adventurous urchin was enjoying a furtive slide in some hidden nook among the bushes. As he watched the dark, solitary figure moving through the desolate wintry waste his involuntary prophecy shot across his mind: 'Something dreadful must surely happen to you.' And at that moment her saw something white rush out of the bushes and come flapping towards her, he saw Thirza start back, and fall on the slippery edge of the pond, and across the meadows a scream came on the frozen air. It was a long while before he could reach the spot, running at his highest speed, and when he arrived the woman was lying half under the scum of churned-up ice and slush at the pond's edge, and something white and ghostly was stealing away through the dusk. Yealmton knew it for a wild swan, wounded by some gunner on the coast, and harbouring among the reeds till it should die; savage and weak with hunger and death-fear, but with strength enough left to do – what it had done.

'Has it ever struck you,' said Vera Durmot to Clovis, 'that one might make a comfortable income by compiling a local almanack, on prophetic lines, like those that the general public buy by the half million?'

'An income, perhaps,' said Clovis, 'but not a comfortable one. The prophet has proverbially a thin sort of time in his own country, and you would be too closely mixed up with the people you were prophesying about to be able to get much comfort out of the job. If the man who foretells tragic happenings for the Crowned Heads of Europe had to meet them at luncheon parties and tea-fights every other day of the week he would not find his business a comfortable one, especially towards the last days of the year, when the tragedies were getting overdue.'

'I should sell it just before the New Year,' said Vera, ignoring the suggestion of possible embarrassment, 'at eighteen pence a copy, and get a friend to type it for me, so that every copy I sold would be clear profit. Everyone would buy it out of curiosity, just to see how many of the predictions would be falsified.'

'Wouldn't it be rather a trying time for you later on,' asked Clovis, 'when the predictions began to "lack confirmation"?'

'The thing would be,' said Vera, 'to arrange your forecast so that it couldn't go very far wrong. I should begin with the prediction that the vicar would preach a moving New Year sermon from a text in Colossians; he has always done so since I can remember, and at his time of life men dislike change. Then one could safely foretell for the month of January that "more than one well-known family in this neighbourhood will be faced with a serious financial outlook that, however, will not develop into actual crisis." Every other head of a family down here discovers about that time of year that his household is living far beyond its income, and that severe retrenchment will be necessary. For April or May or thereabouts I should hint that one of the Dibcuster girls would make the happiest choice of her life. There are eight of them, and it's really time that one of the family married or went on the stage or took to writing worldly novels.'

'They have never done anything of the kind within human memory,' objected Clovis.

'One must take some risks,' said Vera. 'I should be on safer ground,' she added, 'in predicting serious servant troubles from February to November. "Some of the best mistresses and house managers in this locality will be faced with vexatious servant difficulties, which will be temporarily tided over."'

'Another safe forecast,' suggested Clovis, 'could be fitted into the dates when there are medal competitions at the golf club. "One or two of the most brilliant local players will encounter extraordinary and persistent bad luck, which will rob them of the deserved guerdon of good play." At least a dozen men will think your prophecies positively inspired.'

Vera made a note of the suggestion.

'I'll let you have an advance copy at half price,' she said; 'on the other hand, I expect you to see that your mother buys one at market rates.'

'She shall buy two,' said Clovis; 'she can give one to Lady Adela, who never buys anything that she can borrow.'

The almanack had a big sale, and most of its predictions came sufficiently near fulfilment to sustain the compiler's claim to prophetic powers of an eighteen-penny standard. One of the Dibcuster girls made up her mind to be a hospital nurse and another of them gave up piano playing, both of which might be considered happy decisions, while the forecast of servant troubles and unmerited bad luck on the golf links received ample confirmation in the annals of the home and the club.

'I don't see how she was to know that I was going to change my cook twice in seven months,' said Mrs Duff, who easily recognised an allusion to herself as one of the best mistresses of the neighbourhood.

'And it's come quite true about phenomenal vegetable products being recorded from a local garden,' said Mrs Openshaw; 'it said "a garden that has long been the admiration of the neighbourhood for its magnificent flowers will this year produce some marvels in the way of vegetables." Our garden is the admiration of everybody, and yesterday Henry brought in some carrots, well, you wouldn't see anything to equal them at a show.'

'Oh, but I think that refers to our garden,' said Mrs Duff, 'it has always been admired for its flowers, and now we've got some Glory of the South parsnips that beat anything I've ever seen. We've taken their measurements, and I got Phyllis to photograph them. I shall certainly buy the almanack if it comes out another year.'

'I've ordered it already,' said Mrs Openshaw; 'after what it foretold about my garden I thought I ought to.'

While the general verdict was in favour of the almanack as an inspired production, or, at any rate, a very fair compilation of successful prediction, there were critics who pointed out that most of the events foretold were of the nature of things that happened in one form or another in any given year.

'I couldn't risk being very definite about any particular event,' said Vera to Clovis towards the end of the twelvemonth; 'as it is I have rather tied myself up over Jocelyn Vanner.

I hinted that the hunting field was not a safe place for her during November and December. It is never a safe place for her at any time, she is always coming off a jump or getting bolted with or something of that sort. And now she has taken alarm at my prediction, and only comes to the meets on foot. Nothing very serious can happen to her under those circumstances.'

'It must be ruining her hunting season,' said Clovis.

'It's ruining the reputation of my almanack,' said Vera; 'it's the one thing that has definitely miscarried. I felt so sure she would have a spill of some sort that could be magnified into a serious accident.'

'I'm afraid I can't offer to ride over her, or incite hounds to tear her to pieces in mistake for a fox,' said Clovis; 'I should earn your undying devotion, but there would be a wearisome fuss about it, and I should have to hunt with another pack in future, and that would be dreadfully inconvenient.'

'As your mother says, you are a mass of selfishness,' commented Vera.

An opportunity for being unselfish occurred to Clovis a day or two later, when he found himself at close quarters with Jocelyn near Bludberry Gate, where hounds were drawing a long woody hollow in search of an elusive fox.

'Scent is poor, and there's an interminable amount of cover,' grumbled Clovis from his saddle; 'we shall be here for hours before we get a fox away.'

'All the more time for you to talk to me,' said Jocelyn archly.

'The question is,' said Clovis darkly, 'whether I ought to be seen talking to you. I may be involving you.'

'Heavens! Involving me in what?' gasped Jocelyn.

'Do you know anything about Bukovina?' Clovis asked with seeming inconsequence.

'Bukovina? It's somewhere in Asia Minor, isn't it – or Central Asia – or is it part of the Balkans?' hazarded Jocelyn; 'I really forget for the moment. Where exactly is it?'

'On the brink of a revolution,' said Clovis impressively; 'that's what I want to warn you about. When I was staying with my aunt in Bucharest' (Clovis invented aunts as lavishly as other people invent golfing experiences) 'I got mixed up in the affair without knowing what I was in for. There was a princess –'

'Ah,' said Jocelyn knowingly, 'there always is a beautiful and alluring princess in these affairs.'

'As plain and boring a woman as one could find in Eastern Europe,' said Clovis; 'one of the sort that call just before lunch and stay till it's time to dress for dinner. Well, it seems that some Romanian Jew is willing to finance the revolution if he can be assured of getting certain mineral concessions. The Jew is cruising in a yacht somewhere off the English coast, and the princess had made up her mind that I was the safest person to convey the concession papers to him. My aunt whispered, "For Heaven's sake agree to what she says or she'll stay on to dinner." At that moment any sacrifice seemed better than that, and so here I am, with my breast pocket bulging with compromising documents, and my life not worth a minute's purchase.'

'But,' said Jocelyn, 'you are safe here in England, aren't you?'

'Do you see that man over there, on the roan?' asked Clovis, pointing to a man with a heavy black moustache, who was probably an auctioneer from a neighbouring town, and at any rate was a stranger to the hunt. 'That man was outside my aunt's house when I escorted the princess to her carriage. He was on the platform of the railway station when I left Bucharest. He was on the landing stage when I arrived in England. I can go nowhere without finding him at my elbow. I was not surprised to see him at the meet this morning.'

'But what can he do to you?' asked Jocelyn tremulously; 'he can't kill you.'

'Not before witnesses, if he can avoid it. The moment hounds find and the field scatters will be his opportunity. He means to have those papers today.'

'But how can he be sure you've got them on you?'

'He can't; I might have slipped them over to you while we were talking. That is why he is trying to make up his mind which of us to go for at the critical moment.'

'Us?' screamed Jocelyn; 'do you mean to say –?'

'I warned you that it was dangerous to be seen talking to me.'

'But this is awful! What am I to do?'

'Slip away into the undergrowth the moment that hounds get moving, and run like a rabbit. It is your only chance, and remember, if you escape, no talking. Many lives will be involved if you breathe a word of what I've told you. My aunt at Bucharest –'

At that moment there was a whimper from hounds down in the hollow, and a general ripple of movement passed through the scattered groups of waiting horsemen. A louder and more assured burst of noise came up from the valley.

'They've found!' cried Clovis and turned eagerly to join in the stampede. A crashing, scrunching noise as of a body rapidly and resolutely forcing its way through birch thicket and dead bracken was all that remained to him of his late companion.

Jocelyn's most intimate friends never knew the exact nature of the deadly peril she had incurred in the hunting field that day, but enough was made known to ensure the almanack a brisk sale at its new price of three shillings.

A SACRIFICE TO NECESSITY

Alicia Pevenly sat on a garden seat in the rose walk at Chopehanger, enjoying the valedictory mildness of a warm October morning, and experiencing the atmosphere of mental complacency that descends on a woman who has breakfasted well, is picturesquely dressed, and has reached forty-two in pleasant insidious stages. The loss of her husband some ten years ago had woven a thread of tender regret into her life-pattern, but for the most part she looked on the world and its ways with placid acquiescent amiability. The income on which she and her seventeen-year-old daughter lived and kept up appearances was small, almost inconveniently small, perhaps, but with due management and a little forethought it sufficed. Contriving and planning gained a certain amount of zest from the fact that there was only such a slender margin of shillings to be manipulated.

'There is all the difference in the world,' Mrs Pevenly would say to herself, 'between being badly off and merely having to be careful.'

Regarding her own personal affairs with a measured tranquillity, she did not let the larger events of the world disturb her peace of mind. She took a warm, but quite impersonal interest, in the marriage of Prince Arthur of Connaught, thereby establishing her claim to be considered a woman with broad sympathies and intelligently in touch with the age in which she lived. On the other hand, she was not greatly stirred by the question whether Ireland should or should not be given home rule, and she was absolutely indifferent as to where the southern frontier of Albania should be drawn or whether it should be drawn at all; if there had ever been a combative strain in her nature it had never been developed.

Mrs Pevenly had finished her breakfast at about half-past nine, by which time her daughter had not put in an appearance; as the hostess and most of the members of the house party were equally late, Beryl's slackness could not be regarded as a social sin, but her mother thought it was a pity to lose so much of the fine October morning. Beryl Pevenly had been described by someone as the 'flapper incarnate', and the label summed her up accurately. Her mother already recognised that she was disposed to be a law unto herself; what she did not yet realise was that Beryl was extremely likely to be a lawgiver to any weaker character with whom she might come into contact.

'She is only a child yet,' Mrs Pevenly would say to herself, forgetting that seventeen and seventy are about the two most despotic ages of human life.

'Ah, finished breakfast at last!' she called out in mock reproof as her daughter came out to join her in the rose walk; 'if you had gone to bed in good time these last two evenings, as I did, you would not be so tired in the mornings. It has been so fresh and charming out here, while all you silly people have been lying in bed. I hope you weren't playing bridge for high stakes, my dear!'

There was a tired defiant look in Beryl's eyes that drew forth the anxious remark.

'Bridge? No, we started with a rubber or two the night before last,' said Beryl, 'but we switched off to baccarat. Rather a mistake for some of us.'

'Beryl, you haven't been losing?' asked Mrs Pevenly with increased anxiety in her voice.

'I lost quite a lot the first evening,' said Beryl, 'and as I couldn't possibly pay back my losses I simply punted the next evening to try and get them back; I've come to the conclusion that baccarat is not my game. I came a bigger cropper on the second evening than on the first.'

'Beryl, this is awful! I've very angry with you. Tell me quickly, how much have you lost?'

Beryl looked at a slip of paper that she was twisting and untwisting in her hands.

'Three hundred and ten the first night, seven hundred and sixteen the second,' she announced.

'Three hundred what?'

'Pounds.'

'Pounds?' screamed the mother; 'Beryl, I don't believe you. Why, that is a thousand pounds!'

'A thousand and twenty-six, to be exact,' said Beryl.

Mrs Pevenly was too frightened to cry.

'Where do you suppose,' she asked, 'that we could raise a thousand pounds, or anything like a thousand pounds? We are living at the top of our income, we are practising all sorts of economies, we simply couldn't subtract a thousand pounds from our little capital. It would ruin us.'

'We should be socially ruined if it got about that we played for stakes that we couldn't or wouldn't pay; no one would ask us anywhere.'

'How came you to do such a dreadful thing?' wailed the mother.

'Oh, it's no use asking those sort of questions,' said Beryl; 'the thing is done. I suppose I inherit a gambling instinct from some of you.'

'You certainly don't,' exclaimed Mrs Pevenly hotly; 'your father never touched cards or cared anything about horse racing, and I don't know one game of cards from another.'

'These things skip a generation sometimes, and come out all the stronger in the next batch,' said Beryl; 'how about that uncle of yours who used to get up a sweepstake every Sunday at school as to which of the books of the Bible the text of the sermon would be taken from? If he wasn't a keen gambler I've never heard of one.'

'Don't let's argue,' faltered the elder woman, 'let's think of what is to be done. How many people do you owe the money to?'

'Luckily it's all due to one person, Ashcombe Gwent,' said Beryl; 'he was doing nearly all the winning on both nights. He's rather a good sort in his way, but unluckily he isn't a bit well off, and one couldn't expect him to overlook the fact that money was owing to him. I fancy he's just as much of an adventurer as we are.'

'We are not adventurers,' protested Mrs Pevenly.

'People who come to stay at country houses and play for stakes that they've no prospect of paying if they lose, are adventurers,' said Beryl, who seemed determined to include her mother in any moral censure that might be applied to her own conduct.

'Have you said anything to him about the difficulty you are in?'

'I have. That's what I've come to tell you about. We had a talk this morning in the billiard room after breakfast. It seems there is just one way out of the tangle. He's inclined to be amorous.'

'Amorous!' exclaimed the mother.

'Matrimonially amorous,' said the daughter; 'in fact, without either of us having guessed it, it appears that he's the victim of an infatuation.'

'He has certainly been polite and attentive,' said Mrs Pevenly; 'he is not a man who says much, but he listens to what one has to say. And do you mean he really wants to marry –?'

'That is exactly what he does want,' said Beryl. 'I don't know that he is the sort of husband that one would rave about, but I gather that he has enough to live on – as much as we're accustomed to, anyhow, and he's quite presentable to look at. The alternative is selling out a big chunk of our little capital; I should have to go and be a governess or type-writer or something, and you would have to do needlework. From just making things do, and paying rounds of visits and having a fairly good time, we should sink suddenly to the position of distressed gentlefolk. I don't know what you think, but I'm inclined to consider that the marriage proposition is the least objectionable.'

Mrs Pevenly took out her handkerchief.

'How old is he?' she asked.

'Oh, thirty-seven or thirty-eight; a year or two older perhaps.'

'Do you like him?'

Beryl laughed.

'He's not in the least my style,' she said.

Mrs Pevenly began to weep.

'What a deplorable situation,' she sobbed; 'what a sacrifice for the sake of a miserable sum of money and social consider-ations! To think that such a tragedy should happen in our family. I've often read about such things in books, a girl being forced to marry a man she didn't care about because of some financial disaster –'

'You shouldn't read such trashy books,' pronounced Beryl.

'But now it's really happening!' exclaimed the mother; 'my own child's life to be sacrificed by marriage to a man years older than herself, whom she doesn't care the least bit about, and because –'

'Look here,' interrupted Beryl. 'I don't seem to have made this clear. It isn't me that he wants to marry. "Flappers" don't appeal to him, he told me. Mature womanhood is his particular line, and it's you that he's infatuated about.'

'Me!'

For the second time that morning Mrs Pevenly's voice rose to a scream.

'Yes, he said you were his ideal, a ripe, sun-warmed peach, delicious and desirable, and a lot of other metaphors that he probably borrowed from Swinburne or Edmund Jones. I told him that under other circumstances I shouldn't have held out much hope of his getting a favourable response from you, but that as we owed him a thousand and twenty-six pounds you would probably consider a matrimonial alliance the most convenient way of discharging the obligation. He's coming out to speak to you himself in a few minutes, but I thought I'd better come and prepare you first.'

'But, my dear –'

'Of course, you hardly know the man, but I don't think that matters. You see, you've been married before and a second husband is always something of an anticlimax. Here is Ashcombe. I think I'd better leave you two together. You must have a lot you want to say to each other.'

The wedding took place quietly some eight weeks later. The presents were costly, if not numerous, and consisted chiefly of a cancelled IOU, the gift of the bridegroom to the bride's daughter.

'I'm in a frightful position,' exclaimed Mrs Duff-Chubleigh, sinking into an armchair and closing her eyes as though to shut out some distressing vision.

'Really? What has happened?' asked Mrs Pallitson, preparing herself to hear some kitchen tragedy.

'The more one tries to make one's house parties a success, the more one seems to court failure,' was the tragic reply.

'I'm sure it's been most enjoyable so far,' said the guest politely; 'weather, of course, one can't count on, but otherwise I can't see anything has gone wrong. I was thinking you were to be congratulated.'

Mrs Duff-Chubleigh laughed harshly and bitterly.

'It was so nice having the Marchioness here,' she said; 'she's dull and she dresses badly, but people in these parts think no end of her, and, of course, it's rather a social score to get hold of her. It counts for a good deal to be in her good graces. And now she talks of leaving us at a moment's notice.'

'Really? That is unfortunate, but I'm sure she'll be sure to leave such a charming –'

'She's not leaving in sorrow,' said the hostess; 'no – in anger.'

'Anger?'

'Bobbie Chermbacon called her, to her face, a moth-eaten old hen. That's not the sort of thing one says to a marchioness, and I told him so afterwards. He said she was only a marchioness by marriage, which is absurd, because, of course, no one is born a marchioness. Anyway, he didn't apologise, and she says she won't stay under the same roof with him.'

'Under the circumstances,' said Mrs Pallitson, promptly, 'I think you might help Mr Chermbacon to choose a nice early train back to town. There's one that goes before lunch, and

I expect his valet could get the packing act done in something under twenty minutes.'

Mrs Duff-Chubleigh rose in silence, went to the door, and carefully closed it. Then she spoke slowly and impressively, with the air of a minister who is asking an economically minded parliament for an increased Navy vote.

'Bobbie Chermbacon is rich, quite rich, and one day he will be very much richer. His aunt can buy motor cars as we might buy theatre tickets, and he will be her chief heir. I am getting on in years, though I may not look it.'

'You don't,' Mrs Pallitson assured her.

'Thank you; still, the fact remains. I'm getting on in years, and though I've a reasonable number of children of my own I've reached that time of life when a woman begins to feel a great longing for a son-in-law. Bobbie told Margaret last night that she had the eyes of a dreaming madonna.'

'Extravagance in language seems to be his besetting characteristic,' said Mrs Pallitson; 'of course,' she continued hastily, 'I don't mean to say that Margaret hasn't the eyes of a dreaming madonna. I think the simile excellent.'

'There are many different kinds of madonna,' said Mrs Duff-Chubleigh.

'Exactly, but it's rather outspoken language for such short acquaintance. As I say, he seems to be a rather outspoken young man.'

'Ah, but he said more than that; he said she reminded him of Gaby What's-her-name, you know, the fascinating actress that the King of Spain admires so much.'

'Portugal,' murmured Mrs Pallitson.

'And he didn't confine himself to saying pretty things,' continued the mother eagerly; 'actions speak stronger than words. He gave her some exquisite orchids to wear at dinner last night. They were from our orchid-house, but, still, he went to the trouble of picking them.'

'That shows a certain amount of devotion,' agreed Mrs Pallitson.

'And he said he adored chestnut hair,' continued Mrs Duff-Chubleigh; 'Margaret's hair is a very beautiful shade of chestnut.'

'He's known her for a very short time,' said Mrs Pallitson.

'It's always been chestnut,' exclaimed Mrs Duff-Chubleigh.

'Oh, I didn't mean that; I meant that the conquest was sudden, not the colour of the hair. These sudden infatuations are often the most genuine, I believe. A man sees someone for the first time, and knows at once that it is the one person he's been looking for.'

'Well, you see the frightful position I'm in. Either the Marchioness leaves in a fury, or I've got to turn Bobbie adrift just as he and Margaret are getting on so very well. It will nip the whole thing in the bud. I didn't sleep a wink last night. I ate nothing for breakfast. If I'm found floating in the carp-pond, you, at least, will know the reason why.'

'It's certainly a dreadful situation,' said Mrs Pallitson; 'how would it be,' she added slowly and reflectively, 'if I were to ask Margaret and Bobbie over to our place for the remainder of the Marchioness' stay? My husband has got a men's party, but we could easily expand it. Out of all your guests you could subtract three without unduly diminishing your number. We could pretend that it was an old arrangement.'

'Do you mind if I kiss you?' asked Mrs Duff-Chubleigh; 'after this we must call each other by our Christian names. Mine is Elizabeth.'

'There I must object,' said Mrs Pallitson, who had submitted to the kiss; 'there is dignity and charm in the name

Elizabeth, but my godparents christened me Celeste. When a woman weighs as much as I do –'

'I'm sure you don't,' exclaimed her hostess, in defiant disregard of logic.

'And inherits a very uncertain temper,' resumed Mrs Pallitson, 'there is a distinct flavour of incongruity in answering to the name Celeste.'

'You are doing a heavenly thing, and I think the name most appropriate; I shall always call you by it.'

'I'm afraid we haven't an orchid-house,' said Mrs Pallitson, 'but there are some rather choice tuberoses in the hothouse.'

'Margaret's favourite flower!' exclaimed Mrs Duff-Chubleigh.

Mrs Pallitson repressed a sigh. She was fond of tuberoses herself.

The day after the transplanting of Bobbie and Margaret, Mrs Duff-Chubleigh was called to the telephone.

'Is that you, Elizabeth?' came the voice of Mrs Pallitson; 'you must have Bobbie back. Don't say it's impossible, you must. The Bishop of Socotra, my husband's uncle, is staying here. Socotra, never mind how it's spelt. Bobbie told him last night what he thought of Christian missions; I've often said the same thing myself, but never to a bishop. Nor have I expressed it in quite such offensive language. The Bishop refuses to stay another night under the same roof as Bobbie. He, the Bishop, is not merely an uncle, but a bachelor uncle, with private means. It's all very well to say he show a tolerant and charitable spirit; charity begins at home, and this is a Colonial Bishop. Socotra, I keep telling you; it doesn't matter where it is, the point is that the Bishop is here, and we can't allow him to leave us in a temper.'

'How about the Marchioness?' shrilled Mrs Duff-Chubleigh at her end of the phone, having first carefully glanced around to see that nobody was within hearing distance of her remarks. 'She's just as important to me as the Bishop of Scooter, or wherever it is, is to you. I don't know why he should take such absurd unreasonable offence because Christian missions were unfavourably criticised; anyone might express an opinion on a subject of that sort, even to a Colonial Bishop. It's a very different thing being called to your face a moth-eaten old hen. I hear she is going to give a hunt ball at Cloudly this winter, and it's quite probable that she'll ask me over there for it. And now you want me to ruin everything and have a most unpleasant contretemps by taking that boy back under my roof. You can't expect it of me. Besides, we can't keep shifting Mr Chermbacon backwards and forwards as though he was the regulator of an erratic clock. What do you say?'

'The Bishop won't stay another night unless Bobbie goes tonight,' came over the phone in hard relentless tones. 'I've told Bobbie he must leave first thing after lunch, and I've ordered the motor to be ready for him. Margaret can follow tomorrow.'

Then there followed a pitiless silence at the Pallitson end of the telephone. Vainly Mrs Duff-Chubleigh rang up again and again, and put the fruitless and despairing question 'Are you there?' to the cold emptiness of unresponsive space. The Pallitsons had cut themselves off.

'The telephone is the coward's weapon,' muttered Mrs Duff-Chubleigh furiously; 'these heavy blonde women are always a mass of selfishness.'

Then she sat down to write a telegram, as a last appeal to Celeste's better feelings.

Am having carp taken out of fish-pond. I can face drowning, but will not be nibbled.

– ELIZABETH.

As a matter of fact Bobbie Chermbacon and the Marchioness travelled up to town by the same train. He had grasped the fact that his presence was not in request at either of the house parties, and she was hurriedly summoned to London, where her husband had entered on the illness which, in a few days, made her a widow and a dowager. Bobbie's enthusiasm for chestnut hair and dreamy madonna eyes did not lead him to repeat his visit to the Duff-Chubleigh household. He spent the winter in Egypt, and some ten months later he married the widowed Marchioness.

Philip Sletherby settled himself down in an almost-empty railway carriage, with the pleasant consciousness of being embarked on an agreeable and profitable pilgrimage. He was bound for Brill Manor, the country residence of his newly achieved acquaintance, Mrs Saltpen-Jago. Honoria Saltpen-Jago was a person of some social importance in London, and of considerable importance and influence in the county of Chalkshire. The county of Chalkshire, or, at any rate, the eastern division of it, was of immediate personal interest to Philip Sletherby; it was held for the Government in the present Parliament by a gentleman who did not intend to seek re-election, and Sletherby was under serious consideration by the party managers as his possible successor. The majority was not a large one, and the seat could not be considered safe for a ministerial candidate, but there was an efficient local organisation, and with luck the seat might be held. The Saltpen-Jago influence was not an item that could be left out of consideration, and the political aspirant had been delighted at meeting Honoria at a small and friendly luncheon party, still more gratified when she had asked him down to her country house for the following Friday-to-Tuesday. He was obviously 'on approval', and if he could secure the goodwill of his hostess he might count on the nomination as an assured thing. If he failed to find favour in her eyes – well, the local leaders would probably cool off in their embryo enthusiasm for him.

Among the passengers dotted about on the platform, awaiting their respective trains, Sletherby espied a club acquaintance, and beckoned him up to the carriage window for a chat.

'Oh, you're staying with Mrs Saltpen-Jago for the weekend, are you? I expect you'll have a good time; she has the reputation of being an excellent hostess. She'll be useful to you, too, if that Parliamentary project – hullo, you're off. Goodbye.'

Sletherby waved goodbye to his friend, pulled up the window, and turned his attention to the magazine lying on his lap. He had scarcely glanced at a couple of pages, however, when a smothered curse caused him to glance hastily at the only other occupant of the carriage. His travelling companion was a young man of about two-and-twenty, with dark hair, fresh complexion, and the blend of smartness and disarray that marks the costume of a 'nut' who is bound on a rustic holiday. He was engaged in searching furiously and ineffectually for some elusive or non-existent object; from time to time he dug a sixpenny bit out of a waistcoat pocket and stared at it ruefully, then recommenced the futile searching operations. A cigarette-case, matchbox, latchkey, silver pencil case and railway ticket were turned out onto the seat beside him, but none of these articles seemed to afford him satisfaction; he cursed again, rather louder than before.

The vigorous pantomime did not draw forth any remark from Sletherby, who resumed his scrutiny of the magazine.

'I say!' exclaimed a young voice presently, 'didn't I hear you say you were going down to stay with Mrs Saltpen-Jago at Brill Manor? What a coincidence! My mater, you know. I'm coming on there on Monday evening, so we shall meet. I'm quite a stranger; haven't seen the mater for six months at least. I was away yachting last time she was in town. I'm Bertie, the second son, you know. I say, it's an awfully lucky coincidence that I should run across someone who knows the mater just at this particular moment. I've done a damned awkward thing.'

'You've lost something, haven't you?' said Sletherby.

'Not exactly, but left behind, which is almost as bad; just as inconvenient, anyway. I've come away without my sovereign-purse, with four quid in it, all my worldly wealth for the moment. It was in my pocket all right, just before I was starting, and then I wanted to seal a letter, and the sovereign-purse happens to have my crest on it, so I whipped it out to stamp the seal with, and, like a double-distilled idiot, I must have left it on the table. I had some silver loose in my pocket, but after I'd paid for a taxi and my ticket I'd only got this forlorn little sixpence left. I'm stopping at a little country inn near Brondquay for three days' fishing; not a soul knows me there, and my weekend bill, and tips, and cab to and from the station, and my ticket on to Brill, that will mount up to two or three quid, won't it? If you wouldn't mind lending me two pound ten, or three for preference, I shall be awfully obliged. It will pull me out of no end of a hole.'

'I think I can manage that,' said Sletherby, after a moment's hesitation.

'Thanks awfully. It's jolly good of you. What a lucky thing for me that I should have chanced across one of the mater's friends. It will be a lesson to me not to leave my exchequer lying about anywhere, when it ought to be in my pocket. I suppose the moral of the whole thing is don't try and convert things to purposes for which they weren't intended. Still, when a sovereign-purse has your crest on it –'

'What is your crest, by the way?' Sletherby asked, carelessly.

'Not a very common one,' said the youth; 'a demi-lion holding a cross-crosslet in its paw.'

'When your mother wrote to me, giving me a list of trains, she had, if I remember rightly, a greyhound courant on her notepaper,' observed Sletherby. There was a tinge of coldness in his voice.

'That is the Jago crest,' responded the youth promptly; 'the demi-lion is the Saltpen crest. We have the right to use both, but I always use the demi-lion, because, after all, we are really Saltpens.'

There was silence for a moment or two, and the young man began to collect his fishing tackle and other belongings from the rack.

'My station is the next one,' he announced.

'I've never met your mother,' said Sletherby suddenly, 'though we've corresponded several times. My introduction to her was through political friends. Does she resemble you at all in feature? I should rather like to be able to pick her out if she happened to be on the platform to meet me.'

'She's supposed to be like me. She has the same dark brown hair and high colour; it runs in her family. I say, this is where I get out.'

'Goodbye,' said Sletherby.

'You've forgotten the three quid,' said the young man, opening the carriage door and pitching his suitcase onto the platform.

'I've no intention of lending you three pounds, or three shillings,' said Sletherby severely.

'But you said –'

'I know I did. My suspicions hadn't been roused then, though I hadn't necessarily swallowed your story. The discrepancy about the crests put me on my guard, notwithstanding the really brilliant way in which you accounted for it. Then I laid a trap for you; I told you that I had never met Mrs Saltpen-Jago. As a matter of fact I met her at lunch on Monday last. She is a pronounced blonde.'

The train moved on, leaving the *soi-disant* cadet of the Saltpen-Jago family cursing furiously on the platform.

'Well, he hasn't opened his fishing expedition by catching a flat,' chuckled Sletherby. He would have an entertaining story to recount at dinner that evening, and his clever little trap would earn him applause as a man of resource and astuteness. He was still telling his adventure in imagination to an attentive audience of dinner guests when the train drew up at his destination. On the platform he was greeted sedately by a tall footman, and noisily by Claude People, KC,[3] who had apparently travelled down by the same train.

'Hullo, Sletherby! You spending the weekend at Brill? Good. Excellent. We'll have a round of golf together tomorrow; I'll give you your revenge for Hoylake. Not a bad course here, as inland courses go. Ah, here we are; here's the car waiting for us, and very nice, too!'

The car that won the KC's approval was a sumptuous-looking vehicle, which seemed to embody the last word in elegance, comfort and locomotive power. Its graceful lines and symmetrical design masked the fact that it was an enormous wheeled structure, combining the features of a hotel lounge and an engine room.

'Different sort of vehicle to the post-chaise in which our grandfathers used to travel, eh?' exclaimed the lawyer appreciatively. And for Sletherby's benefit he began running over the chief points of perfection in the fitting and mechanism of the car.

Sletherby heard not a single word, noted not one of the details that were being expounded to him. His eyes were fixed on the door panel, on which were displayed two crests: a greyhound courant and a demi-lion holding in its paw a cross-crosslet.

The KC was not the sort of man to notice an absorbed silence on the part of a companion. He had been silent himself for nearly an hour in the train, and his tongue was making up for lost time. Political gossip, personal anecdote and general observation flowed from him in an uninterrupted stream as the car sped along the country roads; from the inner history of the Dublin labour troubles and the private life of the Prince Designate of Albania he progressed with an easy volubility to an account of an alleged happening at the ninth hole at Sandwich, and a verbatim report of a remark made by the Duchess of Pathshire at a Tango tea. Just as the car turned in at the Brill entrance gates the KC captured Sletherby's attention by switching his remarks to the personality of their hostess.

'Brilliant woman, level-headed, a clear thinker, knows exactly when to take up an individual or a cause, exactly when to let him or it drop. Influential woman, but spoils herself and her chances by being too restless. No repose. Good appearance, too, till she made that idiotic change.'

'Change?' queried Sletherby, 'what change?'

'What change? You don't mean to say – Oh, of course, you've only known her just lately. She used to have beautiful dark brown hair, which went very well with her fresh complexion; then one day, about five weeks ago, she electrified everybody by appearing as a brilliant blonde. Quite ruined her looks. Here we are. I say, what's the matter with you? You look rather ill.'

It was early February and the hour was somewhere about two in the morning. Most of the house party had retired to bed. Lucien Wattleskeat had merely retired to his bedroom, where he sat over the still vigorous old age of a fire, balancing the entries in his bridge book. They worked out at seventy-eight shillings on the right side, as the result of two evenings' play, which was not so bad, considering that the stakes had been regrettably low.

Lucien was a young man who regarded himself with an undemonstrative esteem, which the undiscerning were apt to mistake for indifference. Several women of his acquaintance were on the lookout for nice girls for him to marry, a vigil in which he took no share.

The atmosphere of the room was subtly tinged with an essence of tuberose, and more strongly impregnated with the odour of wood-fire smoke. Lucien noticed this latter circumstance as he finished his bridge audit, and also noticed that the fire in the grate was not a wood one, neither was it smoking.

A stronger smell of smoke blew into the room a moment later as the door opened, and Major Boventry, pyjama-clad and solemnly excited, stood in the doorway.

'The house is on fire!' he exclaimed.

'Oh,' said Lucien, 'is that it? I thought perhaps you had come to talk to me. If you would shut the door the smoke wouldn't pour in so.'

'We ought to do something,' said the Major with conviction.

'I hardly know the family,' said Lucien, 'but I suppose one will be expected to be present, even though the fire does not appear to be in this wing of the house.'

'It may spread to here,' said the Major.

'Well, let's go and look at it,' assented Lucien, 'though it's against my principles to meet trouble halfway.'

'Grasp your nettle, that's what I say,' observed Boventry.

'In this case, Major, it's not our nettle,' retorted Lucien, carefully shutting the bedroom door behind him.

In the passage they encountered Canon Clore, arrayed in a dressing gown of Albanian embroidery, which might have escaped remark in a *Te Deum* service in the Cathedral of the Assumption at Moscow, but which looked out of place in the corridor of an English country house. But then, as Lucien observed to himself, at a fire one can wear anything.

'The house is on fire,' said the Canon, with the air of one who lends dignity to a fact by according it gracious recognition.

'It's in the east wing, I think,' said the Major.

'I suppose it is another case of suffragette militancy,' said the Canon. 'I am in favour of women having the vote myself, even if, as some theologians assert, they have no souls. That, indeed, would furnish an additional argument for including them in the electorate, so that all sections of the community, the soulless and the souled, might be represented, and, being in favour of the female vote, I am naturally in favour of militant means to achieve it. Belonging as I do to a Church Militant, I should be inconsistent if I professed to stand aghast at militant methods in vote-winning warfare. But, at the same time, I cannot resist pointing out that the women who are using violent means to wring the vote-right from a reluctant legislature are destroying the value of the very thing for which they are struggling. A vote is of no conceivable consequence to anybody unless it carries with it the implicit understanding that majority rule is the settled order of the day, and the militants are actively engaged in demonstrating that any minority armed with a box of matches and a total disregard of consequences can force its opinions and its wishes on an indifferent or hostile community. It is not merely manor houses they are destroying, but the whole fabric of government by ballot box.'

'Oughtn't we to be doing something about the fire?' said Major Boventry.

'I was going to suggest something of the sort myself,' said the Canon stiffly.

'Tomorrow may be too late, as the advertisements in the newspapers say,' observed Lucien.

In the hall they met their hostess, Mrs Gramplain.

'I'm so glad you have come,' she said; 'servants are so little help in an emergency of this kind. My husband has gone off in the car to summon the fire brigade.'

'Haven't you telephoned to them?' asked the Major.

'The telephone unfortunately is in the east wing,' said the hostess; 'so is the telephone book. Both are being devoured by the flames at this moment. It makes one feel dreadfully isolated. Now if the fire had only broken out in the west wing instead, we could have used the telephone and had the fire engines here by now.'

'On the other hand,' objected Lucien, 'Canon Clore and Major Boventry and myself would probably have met with the fate that has overtaken the telephone book. I think I prefer the present arrangement.'

'The butler and most of the other servants are the dining room, trying to save the Raeburns and the alleged van Dyck,'[4] continued Mrs Gramplain, 'and in that little room on the first landing, cut off from us by the cruel flames, is my poor darling Eva – Eva of the golden hair. Will none of you save her?'

'Who is Eva of the golden hair?' asked Lucien.

'My daughter,' said Mrs Gramplain.

'I didn't know you had a daughter,' said Lucien, 'and really I don't think I can risk my life to save someone I've never met or even heard about. You see, my life is not only wonderful and beautiful to myself, but if my life goes, nothing else really matters – to me. I don't suppose you can realise that, to me, the whole world as it exists today, the Ulster problem, the Albanian tangle, the Kikuyu controversy,[5] the wide field of social reform and Antarctic exploration, the realms of finance, and research and international armaments, all this varied and crowded and complex world, all comes to a complete and absolute end the moment my life is finished. Eva might be snatched from the flames and live to be the grandmother of brilliant and charming men and women; but, as far as I should be concerned, she and they would no more exist than a vanished puff of cigarette smoke or a dissolved soda-water bubble. And if, in losing my life, I am to lose her life and theirs, as far as I personally am concerned with them, why on earth should I, personally, risk my life to save hers and theirs?'

'Major Boventry,' exclaimed Mrs Gramplain, 'you are not clever, but you are a man with honest human feelings. I have only known you for a few hours, but I am sure you are the man I take you for. You will not let my Eva perish.'

'Lady,' said the Major stumblingly, 'I would gladly give my life to rescue your Eva, or anybody's Eva for the matter of that, but my life is not mine to give. I am engaged to the sweetest little woman in the world. I am everything to her. What would my poor little Mildred say if they brought her news that I had cast away my life in an endeavour, perhaps fruitless, to save some unknown girl in a burning country house?'

'You are like all the rest of them,' said Mrs Gramplain bitterly; 'I thought that you, at least, were stupid. It shows how rash it is to judge a man by his bridge-play. It has been like this all my life,' she continued in dull, level tones; 'I was married, when little more than a child, to my husband, and there has never been any real bond of affection between us. We have been polite and considerate to one another, nothing more. I sometimes think that if we had had a child things might have been different.'

'But – your daughter Eva?' queried the Canon, and the two other men echoed his question.

'I have never had a daughter,' said the woman quietly, yet, amid the roar and crackle of the flames, her voice carried, so that not a syllable was lost. 'Eva is the outcome of my imagination. I so much wanted a little girl, and at last I came to believe that she really existed. She grew up, year by year, in my mind, and when she was eighteen I painted her portrait, a beautiful young girl with masses of golden hair. Since that moment the portrait has been Eva. I have altered it a little with the changing years – she is twenty-one now – and I have repainted her dress with every incoming fashion. On her last birthday I painted her a pair of beautiful diamond earrings. Every day I have sat with her for an hour or so, telling her my thoughts, or reading to her. And now she is there, alone with the flames and the smoke, unable to stir, waiting for the deliverance that does not come.'

'It is beautiful,' said Lucien; 'it is the most beautiful thing I ever heard.'

'Where are you going?' asked his hostess, as the young man moved towards the blazing staircase of the east wing.

'I am going to try and save her,' he answered; 'as she has never existed, my death cannot compromise her future existence. I shall go into nothingness, and she, as far as I am concerned, will go into nothingness too; but then she has never been anything else.'

'But your life, your beautiful life?'

'Death in this case, is more beautiful.'

The Major started forward.

'I am going too,' he said simply.

'To save Eva?' cried the woman.

'Yes,' he said; 'my little Mildred will not grudge me to a woman who has never existed.'

'How well he reads our sex,' murmured Mrs Gramplain, 'and yet how badly he plays bridge!'

The two men went side by side up the blazing staircase, the slender young figure in the well-fitting dinner jacket and the thick-set military man in striped pyjamas of an obvious Swan & Edgar pattern. Down in the hall below them stood the woman in her pale wrapper, and the Canon in his wonderful-hued Albanian-work dressing-gown, looking like the arch-priests of some strange religion presiding at a human sacrifice.

As the rescue party disappeared into the roaring cavern of smoke and flames, the butler came into the hall, bearing with him one of the Raeburns.

'I think I hear the clanging of the fire engines, ma'am,' he announced.

Mrs Gramplain continued staring at the spot where the two men had disappeared.

'How stupid of me!' she said presently to the Canon. 'I've just remembered I sent Eva to Exeter to be cleaned. Those two men have lost their lives for nothing.'

'They have certainly lost their lives,' said the Canon.

'The irony of it all,' said Mrs Gramplain, 'the tragic irony of it all!'

'The real irony of the affair lies in the fact that it will be instrumental in working a social revolution of the utmost magnitude,' said the Canon. 'When it becomes known, through the length and breadth of the land, that an army officer and a young ornament of the social world have lost their lives in a country-house fire, started by suffragette incendiarism, the conscience of the country will be aroused, and people will cry out that the price is too heavy to pay. The militants will be in worse odour than ever, but, like the Importunate Widow,[6] they will get their way. Over the charred bodies of Major Boventry and Lucien Wattleskeat the banners of progress and enfranchisement will be carried forward to victory, and the mothers of the nation will henceforth take their part in electing the Mother of Parliaments. England will range herself with Finland and other enlightened countries that have already admitted women to the labours, honours, and responsibilities of the polling booth. In the early hours of this February morning a candle has been lighted…'

'The fire was caused by an over-heated flue, and not by suffragettes, sir,' interposed the butler.

At that moment a scurry of hoofs and a clanging of bells, together with the hoot of a motor-horn, were heard above the roaring of the flames.

'The fire brigade!' exclaimed the Canon.

'The fire brigade and my husband,' said Mrs Gramplain, in her dull level voice; 'it will all begin over again now, the old life, the old unsatisfying weariness, the old monotony; nothing will be changed.'

'Except the east wing,' said the Canon gently.

THE MIRACLE MERCHANT

Characters

MRS BEAUWHISTLE
LOUIS COURCET, *her nephew*
JANE MARTLET
STURRIDGE, MRS BEAUWHISTLE'S *butler*
PAGE BOY

Hall-sitting room in MRS BEAUWHISTLE'S *country house. French window right. Doors right centre and mid-centre. Staircase left centre. Door left. Long table centre of stage, towards footlights, set with breakfast service. Chairs at table. Writing table and chair right of stage. Small hall table back of stage. Wooden panelling below staircase hung with swords, daggers, etc., in view of audience. Stand with golf clubs, etc. left.*

MRS BEAUWHISTLE *seated at writing table; she has had her breakfast. Enter* LOUIS *down staircase.*

LOUIS: Good morning, Aunt. [*He inspects the breakfast dishes.*]

MRS BEAUWHISTLE: Good morning, Louis.

LOUIS: Where is Miss Martlet? [*Helps himself from dish.*]

MRS BEAUWHISTLE: She finished her breakfast a moment ago.

LOUIS: [*sits down*]. I'm glad we're alone; I wanted to ask you – [*Enter* STURRIDGE *left with coffee, which he places on table and withdraws.*] – I wanted to ask you –

MRS BEAUWHISTLE: Whether I could lend you twenty pounds I suppose?

LOUIS: As a matter of fact I was only going to ask for fifteen. Perhaps twenty would sound better.

Mrs Beauwhistle: The answer is the same in either case, and it's no. I couldn't even lend you five. You see I've had no end of extra expenses just lately –

Louis: My dear aunt, please don't give reasons. A charming woman should always be unreasonable, it's part of her charm. Just say, 'Louis, I love you very much, but I'm damned if I lend you any more money.' I should understand perfectly.

Mrs Beauwhistle: Well, we'll take it as said. I've just had a letter from Dora Bittholz, to say she is coming on Thursday.

Louis: This next Thursday? I say, that's rather awkward isn't it?

Mrs Beauwhistle: Why awkward?

Louis: Jane Martlet has only been here six days and she never stays less than a fortnight, even when she's asked definitely for a week. You'll never get her out of the house by Thursday.

Mrs Beauwhistle: But why should I? She and Dora are good friends, aren't they? They used to be.

Louis: Used to be, yes; that is what makes them such bitter enemies now. Each feels that she has nursed a viper in her bosom. Nothing fans the flame of human resentment so much as the discovery that one's bosom has been utilised as a snake sanatorium.

Mrs Beauwhistle: But why are they enemies? What have they quarrelled about? Some man I suppose.

Louis: No. A hen has come between them.

Mrs Beauwhistle: A hen! What hen?

Louis: It was a bronze Leghorn or some such exotic breed, and Dora sold it to Jane at a rather exotic price. They both go in for poultry breeding you know.

Mrs Beauwhistle: If Jane agreed to give the price I don't see what there was to quarrel about –

Louis: Well, you see, the bird turned out to be an abstainer from the egg habit, and I'm told that the letters that passed between the two women were a revelation as to how much abuse could be got onto a sheet of notepaper.

Mrs Beauwhistle: How ridiculous. Couldn't some of their friends compose the quarrel?

Louis: It would have been rather like composing the storm music of a Wagner opera. Jane was willing to take back some of her most libellous remarks if Dora would take back the hen.

Mrs Beauwhistle: And wouldn't she?

Louis: Not she. She said that would be owning herself in the wrong, and you know that Dora would never, under any circumstances, own herself in the wrong. She would as soon think of owning a slum property in Whitechapel as do that.

Mrs Beauwhistle: It will be a most awkward situation, having them both under my roof at the same time. Do you suppose they won't speak to one another?

Louis: On the contrary, the difficulty will be to get them to leave off. Their descriptions of each other's conduct and character have hitherto been governed by the fact that only four ounces of plain speaking can be sent through the post for a penny.

Mrs Beauwhistle: What is to be done? I can't put Dora off, I've already postponed her visit once, and nothing short of a miracle would make Jane leave before her self-allotted fortnight is over.

Louis: I don't mind trying to supply a miracle at short notice – miracles are rather in my line.

Mrs Beauwhistle: My dear Louis, you'll be clever if you get Jane out of this house before Thursday.

LOUIS: I shall not only be clever, I shall be rich; in sheer gratitude you will say to me, 'Louis, I love you more than ever, and here are the twenty pounds we were speaking about.'

[*Enter* JANE *door centre.*]

JANE: Good morning Louis.
LOUIS [*rising*]: Good morning Jane.
JANE: Go on with your breakfast; I've had mine but I'll just have a cup of coffee to keep you company. [*Helps herself.*] Is there any toast left?
LOUIS: Sturridge is bringing some. Here it comes.

[STURRIDGE *enters left with toast rack.* JANE *seats herself and is helped to toast; she takes three pieces.*]

JANE: Isn't there any butter?
STURRIDGE: Your sleeve is in the butter, miss.
JANE: Oh, yes.

[*Helps herself generously. Exit* STURRIDGE *left.*]

MRS BEAUWHISTLE: Jane dear, I see the Mackenzie–Hubbard wedding is on Thursday next. St Peter's, Eaton Square, such a pretty church for weddings. I suppose you'll be wanting to run away from us to attend it. You were always such friends with Louisa Hubbard, it would hardly do for you not to turn up.
JANE: Oh I'm not going to bother to go all that way for a silly wedding, much as I like Louisa; I shall go and stay with her for several weeks after she's come back from her

66

honeymoon. [LOUIS *grins across at his aunt.*] I don't see any honey!

LOUIS: Your other sleeve's in the honey.

JANE: Bother, so it is. [*Helps herself liberally.*]

MRS BEAUWHISTLE [*rising*]: Well, I must leave you and go and do some gardening. Ring for anything you want, Jane.

JANE: Thank you, I'm all right.

[*Exit* MRS BEAUWHISTLE, *by French window right.*]

LOUIS [*pushing back his chair*]: Do you mind my smoking?

JANE [*still eating heartily*]: Not at all. [*Enter* STURRIDGE *with tray, left, as if to clear away breakfast things. Places tray on side table, back centre, and is about to retire.*] Oh, I say, can I have some more hot milk? This is nearly cold.

[STURRIDGE *takes jug and exit left.* LOUIS *looks fixedly after him. Seats himself near* JANE *and stares solemnly at the floor.*]

LOUIS: Servants are a bit of a nuisance.

JANE: Servants a nuisance! I should think they are! The trouble I have in getting suited you would hardly believe. But I don't see what you have to complain of – your aunt is so wonderfully lucky in her servants. Sturridge for instance – he's been with her for years and I'm sure he's a jewel as butlers go.

LOUIS: That's just the trouble. It's when servants have been with you for years that they become a really serious nuisance. The other sort, the here today and gone tomorrow lot, don't matter – you've simply got to replace them. It's the stayers and the jewels that are the real worry.

JANE: But if they give satisfaction –

67

LOUIS: That doesn't prevent them from giving trouble. As it happens, I was particularly thinking of Sturridge when I made the remark about servants being a nuisance.

JANE: The excellent Sturridge a nuisance! I can't believe it.

LOUIS: I know he is excellent and my aunt simply couldn't get along without him. But his very excellence has had an effect on him.

JANE: What effect?

LOUIS [*solemnly*]: Have you ever considered what it must be like to go on unceasingly doing the correct thing in the correct manner in the same surroundings for the greater part of a lifetime? To know and ordain and superintend exactly what silver and glass and table linen shall be used and set out on what occasions, to have pantry and cellar and plate-cupboard under a minutely devised and undeviating administration, to be noiseless, impalpable, omnipresent, infallible?

JANE [*with conviction*]: I should go mad.

LOUIS: Exactly. Mad.

[*Enter* STURRIDGE *left with milk jug which he places on table and exit left.*]

JANE: But – Sturridge hasn't gone mad.

LOUIS: On most points he's thoroughly sane and reliable, but at times he is subject to the most obstinate delusions.

JANE: Delusions – what sort of delusions? [*She helps herself to more coffee.*]

LOUIS: Unfortunately they usually centre round someone staying in the house; that is where the awkwardness comes in. For instance, he took it into his head that Matilda Shering-ham, who was here last summer, was the prophet Elijah.

JANE: The prophet Elijah! The man who was fed by ravens?

LOUIS: Yes, it was the ravens that particularly impressed Sturridge's imagination. He was rather offended, it seems, at the idea that Matilda should have her private catering arrangements and he declined to compete with the birds in any way; he wouldn't allow any tea to be sent up to her in the morning and when he waited at table he passed her over altogether in handing round the dishes. Poor Matilda could scarcely get anything to eat.

JANE: How horrible! How very horrible! Whatever did you do?

LOUIS: It was judged best for her to cut her visit short. [*With emphasis.*] In a case of that kind it was the only thing to be done.

JANE: I shouldn't have done that. [*Cuts herself some bread and butters it.*] I should have humoured him in some way. I should have said the ravens were moulting. I certainly shouldn't have gone away.

LOUIS: It's not always wise to humour people when they get these ideas into their heads. There's no knowing to what lengths they might go.

JANE: You don't mean to say Sturridge might be dangerous?

LOUIS: One can never be certain. Now and then he gets some idea about a guest that might take an unfortunate turn. That is what is worrying me at the present moment.

JANE [*excitedly*]: Why, has he taken some fancy about me?

LOUIS [*who has taken a putter out of the stand, left and is polishing it with an oil rag*]: He has.

JANE: No, really? Who on earth does he think I am?

LOUIS: Queen Anne.

JANE: Queen Anne! What an idea! But anyhow there's nothing dangerous about her; she's such a colourless personality. No one could feel very strongly about Queen Anne.

LOUIS [*sternly*]: What does posterity chiefly say about her?

JANE: The only thing I can remember about her is the saying 'Queen Anne's dead.'

LOUIS: Exactly. Dead.

JANE: Do you mean that he takes me for the *ghost* of Queen Anne?

LOUIS: Ghost! Dear no. Who ever heard of a ghost that came down to breakfast and ate kidneys and toast and honey with a healthy appetite? No, it's the fact of you being so very much alive and flourishing that perplexes and irritates him.

JANE [*anxiously*]: Irritates him?

LOUIS: Yes. All his life he has been accustomed to look on Queen Anne as the personification of everything that is dead and done with, 'as dead as Queen Anne' you know, and now he has to fill your glass at lunch and dinner and listen to your accounts of the gay time you had at the Dublin horse show, and naturally he feels that there is something scandalously wrong somewhere.

JANE [*with increased anxiety*]: But he wouldn't be downright hostile to me on that account, would he! Not violent?

LOUIS [*carelessly*]: I didn't get really alarmed about it till last night, when he was bringing in the coffee. I caught him scowling at you with a very threatening look and muttering things about you.

JANE: What things?

LOUIS: That you ought to be dead long ago and that some-one should see to it, and that if no one else did he would. [*Cheerfully.*] That's why I mentioned the matter to you.

JANE: This is awful! Your aunt must be told about it at once.

LOUIS: My aunt mustn't hear a word about it. It would upset her dreadfully. She relies on Sturridge for everything.

JANE: But he might kill me at any moment!

LOUIS: Not at any moment; he's busy with the silver all the afternoon.

JANE: What a frightful situation to be in, with a mad butler dangling over one's head.

LOUIS: Of course it's only a temporary madness; perhaps if you were to cut your visit short and come to us some time later in the year he might have forgotten all about Queen Anne.

JANE: Nothing would induce me to cut short my visit. You must keep a sharp look out on Sturridge and be ready to intervene if he gets violent. Probably we are both exaggerating things a bit. [*Rising.*] I must go and write some letters in the morning room. Mind, keep an eye on the man. [*Exit door right centre.*]

LOUIS [*savagely*]: *Quel type!*[7]

[*Enter* MRS BEAUWHISTLE *by French window right.*]

MRS BEAUWHISTLE: Can't find my gardening gloves anywhere. I suppose they are where I left them; it's a way my things have. [*Rummages in drawer of table back centre.*] They are. [*Produces gloves from drawer.*] And how is your miracle doing, Louis?

LOUIS: Rotten! I've invented all sorts of excellent reasons for stimulating the migration instinct in that woman, but you might as well try to drive away an attack of indigestion by talking to it.

MRS BEAUWHISTLE: Poor Louis! I'm afraid Jane's staying powers are superior to any amount of hustling that you can bring to bear. [*Enter* STURRIDGE *left; he begins clearing breakfast things.*] I could have told you from the first that you were engaged on a wild goose chase.

LOUIS: Chase! You can't chase a thing that refuses to budge. One of the first conditions of the chase is that the thing you are chasing should run away.

MRS BEAUWHISTLE [*laughing*]: That's a condition that Jane will never fulfil.

[*Exit through window right.* LOUIS *continues cleaning golf club, then suddenly stops and looks reflectively at* STURRIDGE, *who is busy with the breakfast things.*]

LOUIS: Where is Miss Martlet?

STURRIDGE: In the morning room, I believe, sir, writing letters.

LOUIS: You see that old basket-hilted sword on the wall?

STURRIDGE: Yes, sir. This big one? [*Points to sword.*]

LOUIS: Miss Martlet wants to copy the inscription on its blade. I wish you would take it to her; my hands are all over oil.

STURRIDGE: Yes, sir. [*Turns to wall where sword is hanging.*]

LOUIS: Take it without the sheath, it will be less trouble.

[STURRIDGE *draws the blade, which is broad and bright and exits by door centre.* LOUIS *stands back under shadow of staircase. Enter* JANE *door right centre, at full run, screams:* 'Louis! Louis! Where are you?' *and rushes up stairs at top speed. Enter* STURRIDGE *door right centre, sword in hand.* LOUIS *steps forward.*]

STURRIDGE: Miss Martlet slipped out of the room, sir, as I came in; I don't think she saw me coming. Seemed in a bit of a hurry.

LOUIS: Perhaps she has a train to catch. Never mind, you can put the sword back. I'll copy out the inscription for her myself later.

[STURRIDGE *returns sword to its place.* LOUIS *continues cleaning putter.* STURRIDGE *carries breakfast tray out by door left. Enter* PAGE, *running full speed down stairs.*]

PAGE: The timetable! Miss Martlet wants to look up a train.

[LOUIS *dashes to drawer of small table centre; he and* PAGE *hunt through contents, throwing gloves, etc., onto floor.*]

LOUIS: Here it is! [PAGE *seizes book, starts to run upstairs,* LOUIS *grabs him by tip of jacket, pulls him back, opens books, searches frantically.*] Here you are. Leaves eleven fifty-five, arrives Charing Cross two-twenty. [PAGE *dashes upstairs with timetable.* LOUIS *flies to speaking tube in wall left, whistles down it.*] Is that you, Tomkins? The car as quick as you can, to catch the eleven fifty-five. Never mind your livery, just as you are.

[*Shuts off tube.* PAGE *dashes down stairs.*]

PAGE: Miss Martlet's golf clubs!

[LOUIS *dashes for them in stand, and gives them to boy.*]

LOUIS: Here, this Tam-o'-shanter is hers – and this motor veil.

[*Gives them to boy.*]

PAGE: She said there was a novel of hers down here.

[LOUIS *goes to writing table where there are six books on shelf and gives them all to* PAGE.]

Louis: Here, take the lot. Fly! [*He pushes the* Page *vigorously up first steps of staircase. Exit* Page. *The sound of books dropping can be heard as he goes.* Louis *dashes round room to see if anything more belonging to* Jane *remains. Looks at his watch; compares it with small clock on writing table. Goes to speaking tube.*] Hullo, is Tomkins there? What? Oh, all right. [*Shuts off tube. Goes to table where coffee pot still remains and pours out cup of coffee, drinks it. Looks again at watch.*]

Sturridge [*enters left*]: The car has come round, sir.

Louis: Good. I'll go and tell Miss Martlet. Will you find my aunt, she's somewhere in the garden, and tell her that Miss Martlet had to leave in a hurry to catch the eleven fifty-five; called away urgently and couldn't stop to say goodbye. Matter of life and death.

Sturridge: Yes, sir.

[*Exit* Sturridge *door left.* Louis *exit up staircase. Enter* Mrs Beauwhistle *by window right. She has a letter in her hand. She looks in at door right centre, returns and calls.* 'Louis – Louis!' *Sound of a motor heard,* Louis *rushes in by door left.*]

Louis [*excitedly*]: How much did you say you'd lend me if I got rid of Jane Martlet?

Mrs Beauwhistle: We needn't get rid of her. Dora has just written to say she can't come this month.

[Louis *collapses into chair.*]

Curtain

A leading French newspaper a few years ago published an imaginary account of the difficulties experienced by Noah in mobilising birds and beasts and creeping things for embarkation in the ark. The arctic animals were the chief embarrassment; the polar bears persistently ate the seals long before the consignment had reached the rendezvous, and while a fresh supply was being sent for certain South American insects, which only live for a few hours, had to be kept alive by artificial respiration. When everything seemed at length to have been got ready, and the last bale of hay and the last hundredweight of birdseed had been taken on board, someone asked, with cold reproach, 'I suppose you know you've forgotten the Australian animals?'

The job of Company Orderly Corporal resembles in some respects the labours of Noah; one can never safely flatter oneself at any given moment that one has got to a temporary end of it. When one has drawn the milk and doled out the margarine, and distributed the letters and parcels, and seen to the whereabouts of migratory tea pails and flat pans and paraded defaulters and off-duty men under the cold scrutiny of the canteen sergeant – and disentangled recruits from messes to which they do not belong – and induced unwilling hut-orderlies to saddle themselves with buckets full of unpeeled potatoes that they neither desire nor deserve – and has begun to think that the moment has arrived in which one may indulge in a cigarette and read a letter – then some detestably thoughtful friend will sidle up to one and say, 'I suppose you know there's the watercress waiting at the cookhouse?'

There are at least two distinct styles in use by those who hold the office of Company Orderly Corporal. One is to stalk at the head of one's hut-orderlies like a masterful rainproof hen on a wet day, followed by a melancholy string of wish-they-had-never-been-hatched chickens; the other is to rush about in a demented fashion, as though one had invented the science of modern camp organisation and had forgotten most of the details.

There are certain golden rules to be observed by the COC who wishes to make a success of his job.

Cultivate an indifference to human suffering; if heaven intended hut-orderlies to be happy you have received no instructions on the point.

Develop your imagination; if the officer of the day remarks on the paleness of a joint of meat, hazard the probable explanation that the beast it was cut from was fed on Sicilian clover, which fattens quickly, but gives a pale appearance; there may be no such thing as Sicilian clover, but one half of the world believes what the other half invents. At any rate, you will get credit for unusual intelligence.

Be kind to those who live in cookhouses.

It has been said that 'great men are lovable for their mistakes'; do not imagine for a moment that this applies, even in a minor degree, to Company Orderly Corporals. If you make the mistake of forgetting to draw the Company's butter till the Company's tea is over, no one will love you or pretend to love you.

A gifted woman writer has observed 'it is an extravagance to do anything that someone else can do better.' Be extravagant.

Of all the labours that fall to the lot of COC the most formidable is the distribution of the postbag. There are about seven men in every hut who are expecting important letters that never seem to reach them, and there are always individuals who glower at you and tell you that they invariably get a letter from home on Tuesday; by Thursday they are firmly convinced that you have set all their relations against them. There was one young man in Hut 3 whose reproachful looks got on my nerves to such an extent that at last I wrote him a letter from his Aunt Agatha, a letter full of womanly counsel and patient reproof, such as any aunt might have been proud to write. Possibly he hasn't got an Aunt Agatha; anyhow, the reproachful look has been replaced by a puzzled frown.

TOBERMORY

It was a chill, rain-washed afternoon of a late August day,
that indefinite season when partridges are still in security or
cold storage, and there is nothing to hunt – unless one is
bounded on the north by the Bristol Channel, in which case
one may lawfully gallop after fat red stags. Lady Blemley's
house party was not bounded on the north by the Bristol
Channel, hence there was a full gathering of her guests round
the tea-table on this particular afternoon. And, in spite of the
blankness of the season and the triteness of the occasion, there
was no trace in the company of that fatigued restlessness that
means a dread of the pianola and a subdued hankering for
auction bridge. The undisguised open-mouthed attention of
the entire party was fixed on the homely negative personality of
Mr Cornelius Appin. Of all her guests, he was the one who had
come to Lady Blemley with the vaguest reputation. Someone
had said he was 'clever', and he had got his invitation in the
moderate expectation, on the part of his hostess, that some
portion at least of his cleverness would be contributed to the
general entertainment. Until teatime that day she had been
unable to discover in what direction, if any, his cleverness lay.
He was neither a wit nor a croquet champion, a hypnotic force
nor a begetter of amateur theatricals. Neither did his exterior
suggest the sort of man in whom women are willing to pardon
a generous measure of mental deficiency. He had subsided
into mere Mr Appin, and the Cornelius seemed a piece of
transparent baptismal bluff. And now he was claiming to have
launched on the world a discovery beside which the invention
of gunpowder, of the printing press, and of steam locomotion
were inconsiderable trifles. Science had made bewildering
strides in many directions during recent decades, but this thing

seemed to belong to the domain of miracle rather than to scientific achievement.

'And do you really ask us to believe,' Sir Wilfrid was saying, 'that you have discovered a means for instructing animals in the art of human speech, and that dear old Tobermory has proved your first successful pupil?'

'It is a problem at which I have worked for the last seventeen years,' said Mr Appin, 'but only during the last eight or nine months have I been rewarded with glimmerings of success. Of course I have experimented with thousands of animals, but latterly only with cats, those wonderful creatures that have assimilated themselves so marvellously with our civilisation while retaining all their highly developed feral instincts. Here and there among cats one comes across an outstanding superior intellect, just as one does among the ruck of human beings, and when I made the acquaintance of Tobermory a week ago I saw at once that I was in contact with a "Beyond-cat" of extraordinary intelligence. I had gone far along the road to success in recent experiments; with Tobermory, as you call him, I have reached the goal.'

Mr Appin concluded his remarkable statement in a voice that he strove to divest of a triumphant inflection. No one said 'Rats,' though Bertie van Tahn's lips moved in a monosyllabic contortion, which probably invoked those rodents of disbelief.

'And do you mean to say,' asked Miss Resker, after a slight pause, 'that you have taught Tobermory to say and understand easy sentences of one syllable?'

'My dear Miss Resker,' said the wonder-worker patiently, 'one teaches little children and savages and backward adults in that piecemeal fashion; when one has once solved the problem of making a beginning with an animal of highly developed intelligence one has no need for those halting methods. Tobermory can speak our language with perfect correctness.'

This time Bertie van Tahn very distinctly said, 'Beyond-rats!' Sir Wilfred was more polite but equally sceptical.

'Hadn't we better have the cat in and judge for ourselves?' suggested Lady Blemley.

Sir Wilfred went in search of the animal, and the company settled themselves down to the languid expectation of witnessing some more or less adroit drawing-room ventriloquism.

In a minute Sir Wilfred was back in the room, his face white beneath its tan and his eyes dilated with excitement.

'By Gad, it's true!'

His agitation was unmistakably genuine, and his hearers started forward in a thrill of wakened interest.

Collapsing into an armchair he continued breathlessly:

'I found him dozing in the smoking room, and called out to him to come for his tea. He blinked at me in his usual way, and I said, "Come on, Toby; don't keep us waiting," and, by Gad! he drawled out in a most horribly natural voice that he'd come when he dashed well pleased! I nearly jumped out of my skin!'

Appin had preached to absolutely incredulous hearers; Sir Wilfred's statement carried instant conviction. A Babel-like chorus of startled exclamation arose, amid which the scientist sat mutely enjoying the first fruit of his stupendous discovery.

In the midst of the clamour Tobermory entered the room and made his way with velvet tread and studied unconcern across the group seated round the tea-table.

A sudden hush of awkwardness and constraint fell on the company. Somehow there seemed an element of embarrassment in addressing on equal terms a domestic cat of acknowledged dental ability.

'Will you have some milk, Tobermory?' asked Lady Blemley in a rather strained voice.

'I don't mind if I do,' was the response, couched in a tone of even indifference. A shiver of suppressed excitement went through the listeners, and Lady Blemley might be excused for pouring out the saucerful of milk rather unsteadily.

'I'm afraid I've spilt a good deal of it,' she said apologetically.

'After all, it's not my Axminster,' was Tobermory's rejoinder.

Another silence fell on the group, and then Miss Resker, in her best district-visitor manner, asked if the human language had been difficult to learn. Tobermory looked squarely at her for a moment and then fixed his gaze serenely on the middle distance. It was obvious that boring questions lay outside his scheme of life.

'What do you think of human intelligence?' asked Mavis Pellington lamely.

'Of whose intelligence in particular?' asked Tobermory coldly.

'Oh, well, mine for instance,' said Mavis with a feeble laugh.

'You put me in an embarrassing position,' said Tobermory, whose tone and attitude certainly did not suggest a shred of embarrassment. 'When your inclusion in this house party was suggested Sir Wilfrid protested that you were the most brainless woman of his acquaintance, and that there was a wide distinction between hospitality and the care of the feeble-minded. Lady Blemley replied that your lack of brainpower was the precise quality that had earned you your invitation, as you were the only person she could think of who might be idiotic enough to buy their old car. You know, the one they call "The Envy of Sisyphus", because it goes quite nicely uphill if you push it.'

Lady Blemley's protestations would have had greater effect if she had not casually suggested to Mavis only that morning that the car in question would be just the thing for her down at her Devonshire home.

Major Barfield plunged in heavily to effect a diversion.

'How about your carryings-on with the tortoiseshell puss up at the stables, eh?'

The moment he had said it everyone realised the blunder.

'One does not usually discuss these matters in public,' said Tobermory frigidly. 'From a slight observation of your ways since you've been in this house I should imagine you'd find it inconvenient if I were to shift the conversation to your own little affairs.'

The panic that ensued was not confined to the Major.

'Would you like to go and see if cook has got your dinner ready?' suggested Lady Blemley hurriedly, affecting to ignore the fact that it wanted at least two hours to Tobermory's dinner-time.

'Thanks,' said Tobermory, 'not quite so soon after my tea. I don't want to die of indigestion.'

'Cats have nine lives, you know,' said Sir Wilfred heartily.

'Possibly,' answered Tobermory; 'but only one liver.'

'Adelaide!' said Mrs Cornett, 'do you mean to encourage that cat to go out and gossip about us in the servants' hall?'

The panic had indeed become general. A narrow ornamental balustrade ran in front of most of the bedroom windows at the Towers, and it was recalled with dismay that this had formed a favourite promenade for Tobermory at all hours, whence he could watch the pigeons – and heaven knew what else besides. If he intended to become reminiscent in his present outspoken strain the effect would be something more than disconcerting. Mrs Cornett, who spent much time at her toilet table, and whose complexion was reputed to be of a nomadic though punctual disposition, looked as ill at ease as the Major. Miss

Scrawen, who wrote fiercely sensuous poetry and led a blameless life, merely displayed irritation; if you are methodical and virtuous in private you don't necessarily want everyone to know it. Bertie van Tahn, who was so depraved at seventeen that he had long ago given up trying to be any worse, turned a dull shade of gardenia white, but he did not commit the error of dashing out of the room like Odo Finsberry, a young gentleman who was understood to be reading for the Church and who was possibly disturbed at the thought of scandals he might hear concerning other people.

Even in a delicate situation like the present, Agnes Resker could not endure to remain long in the background.

'Why did I ever come down here?' she asked dramatically.

Tobermory immediately accepted the opening.

'Judging by what you said to Mrs Cornett on the croquet lawn yesterday, you were out of food. You described the Blemleys as the dullest people to stay with that you knew, but said they were clever enough to employ a first-rate cook; otherwise they'd find it difficult to get anyone to come down a second time.'

'There's not a word of truth in it! I appeal to Mrs Cornett –' exclaimed the discomfited Agnes.

'Mrs Cornett repeated your remark afterwards to Bertie van Tahn,' continued Tobermory, 'and said, "That woman is a regular hunger marcher; she'd go anywhere for four square meals a day," and Bertie van Tahn said –'

At this point the chronicle mercifully ceased. Tobermory had caught a glimpse of the big yellow tom from the Rectory working his way through the shrubbery towards the stable wing. In a flash he had vanished through the open French window.

With the disappearance of his too-brilliant pupil Cornelius Appin found himself beset by a hurricane of bitter upbraiding, anxious enquiry, and frightened entreaty. The responsibility for the situation lay with him, and he must prevent matters from becoming worse. Could Tobermory impart his dangerous gift to other cats? was the first question he had to answer. It was possible, he replied, that he might have initiated his intimate friend the stable puss into his new accomplishment, but it was unlikely that his teaching could have taken a wider range as yet.

'Then,' said Mrs Cornett, 'Tobermory may be a valuable cat and a great pet; but I'm sure you'll agree, Adelaide, that both he and the stable cat must be done away with without delay.'

'You don't suppose I've enjoyed the last quarter of an hour, do you?' said Lady Blemley bitterly. 'My husband and I are very fond of Tobermory – at least, we were before this horrible accomplishment was infused into him; but now, of course, the only thing is to have him destroyed as soon as possible.'

'We can put some strychnine in the scraps he always gets at dinner-time,' said Sir Wilfred, 'and I will go and drown the stable cat myself. The coachman will be very sore at losing his pet, but I'll say a very catching form of mange has broken out in both cats and we're afraid of it spreading to the kennels.'

'But my great discovery!' expostulated Mr Appin; 'after all my years of research and experiment –'

'You can go and experiment on the shorthorns at the farm, who are under proper control,' said Mrs Cornett, 'or the elephants at the Zoological Gardens. They're said to be highly intelligent, and they have this recommendation, that they don't come creeping about our bedrooms and under chairs, and so forth.'

An archangel ecstatically proclaiming the millennium, and then finding that it clashed unpardonably with Henley and would have to be indefinitely postponed, could hardly have felt more crestfallen than Cornelius Appin at the reception of his wonderful achievement. Public opinion, however, was against him – in fact, had the general voice been consulted on the subject it is probable that a strong minority vote would have been in favour of including him in the strychnine diet.

Defective train arrangements and a nervous desire to see matters brought to a finish prevented an immediate dispersal of the party, but dinner that evening was not a social success. Sir Wilfred had had rather a trying time with the stable cat and subsequently with the coachman. Agnes Resker ostentatiously limited her repast to a morsel of dry toast, which she bit as though it were a personal enemy, while Mavis Pellington maintained a vindictive silence throughout the meal. Lady Blemley kept up a flow of what she hoped was conversation, but her attention was fixed on the doorway. A plateful of carefully dosed fish scraps was in readiness on the sideboard, but the sweets and savoury and dessert went their way, and no Tobermory appeared in the dining room or kitchen.

The sepulchral dinner was cheerful compared with the subsequent vigil in the smoking room. Eating and drinking had at least supplied a distraction and cloak to the prevailing embarrassment. Bridge was out of the question in the general tension of nerves and tempers, and after Odo Finsberry had given a lugubrious rendering of 'Melisande in the Wood'[8] to a frigid audience, music was tacitly avoided. At eleven the servants went to bed, announcing that the small window in the pantry had been left open as usual for Tobermory's private use. The guests read steadily through the current batch of magazines, and fell back gradually on the 'Badminton Library' and bound volumes of *Punch*.[9] Lady Blemley made periodic visits to the pantry, returning each time with an expression of listless depression that forestalled questioning.

At two o'clock Bertie van Tahn broke the dominating silence.

'He won't turn up tonight. He's probably in the local newspaper office at the present moment, dictating the first instalment of his reminiscences. Lady What's-her-name's book won't be in it. It will be the event of the day.'

Having made this contribution to the general cheerfulness, Bertie van Tahn went to bed. At long intervals the various members of the house party followed his example.

The servants taking round the early tea made a uniform announcement in reply to a uniform question. Tobermory had not returned.

Breakfast was, if anything, a more unpleasant function than dinner had been, but before its conclusion the situation was relieved. Tobermory's corpse was brought in from the shrubbery, where a gardener had just discovered it. From the bites on his throat and the yellow fur that coated his claws it was evident that he had fallen in unequal combat with the big tom from the Rectory.

By midday most of the guests had quitted the Towers, and after lunch Lady Blemley had sufficiently recovered her spirits to write an extremely nasty letter to the Rectory about the loss of her valuable pet.

Tobermory had been Appin's one successful pupil, and he was destined to have no successor. A few weeks later an elephant in the Dresden Zoological Garden, which had shown no previous signs of irritability, broke loose and killed an Englishman who had apparently been teasing it. The victim's name was variously reported in the papers as Oppin and Eppelin, but his front name was faithfully rendered Cornelius.

'If he was trying German irregular verbs on the poor beast,' said Bertie van Tahn, 'he deserved all he got.'

NOTES

1. A member of The Society of Writers to Her Majesty's Signet, a private society of Scottish solicitors.

2. William Pitt the Elder (1708–79) and the Younger (1759–1806) and Thomas Henry Burke (1829–82) were British statesmen; Charles Maurice de Talleyrand was a French statesman.

3. King's Counsel.

4. Sir Henry Raeburn (1756–1823), portrait painter; Sir Anthony van Dyck (1599–1641), painter, and one of the great masters of portraiture.

5. 'The Ulster problem' refers to the question of home rule for Ireland; 'the Albanian tangle' refers to the competing interests in Albania after it was ceded by the Ottoman Empire in 1912; and 'the Kikuyu controversy' refers to the most active ethnic group during the fight for Kenyan independence.

6. The widow in Jesus' parable, whose request was answered because of her persistence (Luke 18:1–8).

7. 'What a sort!' (French)

8. Song by Ethel Clifford and Alma Goetz.

9. The Badminton Library of Sports and Pastimes was a series of books covering various leisure activities, published between 1885 and 1902; the satirical magazine *Punch* ran from 1841 to 2002.

BIOGRAPHICAL NOTE

Hector Hugh Munro was born in Akyab, Myanmar, in 1870, the son of an inspector-general for the Burmese police. His mother was killed in 1872, and he and his brother and sister were brought up in England by his grandmother and aunts. He was educated at Pencarwick School in Exmouth and the Bedford Grammar School.

In 1893 Munro joined the Burmese police, but three years later his health forced his resignation and return to England, where he began his career as a journalist, writing for newspapers such as the *Westminster Gazette*, the *Daily Express*, *Bystander*, the *Morning Post* and *Outlook*.

In 1900 Munro's first book was published, *The Rise of the Russian Empire*, which was modelled on Gibbon's *The Decline and Fall of the Roman Empire*. His first book as Saki, *The Westminster Alice*, appeared in 1902.

From 1902 to 1908 Munro worked as a foreign correspondent for the *Morning Post* before settling in London. On the eve of the First World War, he wrote the novel *When William Came*, imagining the eponymous German emperor conquering Britain.

Although officially over age Munro joined the Army at the start of the First World War as an ordinary soldier, refusing a commission. In 1916, while sheltering in a shell crater near Beaumont-Hamel, in France, he was killed by a German sniper.

After his death Munro's sister Ethel destroyed most of his papers and wrote her own account of their childhood. Munro's pen name, Saki, is thought to be a reference to the cupbearer in the *Rubáiyát of Omar Khayyam*.

SELECTED TITLES FROM HESPERUS PRESS

Author	Title	Foreword writer
Pedro Antonio de Alarcón	*The Three-Cornered Hat*	
Louisa May Alcott	*Behind a Mask*	Doris Lessing
Dante Alighieri	*New Life*	Louis de Bernières
Dante Alighieri	*The Divine Comedy: Inferno*	Ian Thomson
Edmondo de Amicis	*Constantinople*	Umberto Eco
Gabriele D'Annunzio	*The Book of the Virgins*	Tim Parks
Pietro Aretino	*The School of Whoredom*	Paul Bailey
Pietro Aretino	*The Secret Life of Nuns*	
Pietro Aretino	*The Secret Life of Wives*	Paul Bailey
Jane Austen	*Lady Susan*	
Jane Austen	*Lesley Castle*	Zoë Heller
Jane Austen	*Love and Friendship*	Fay Weldon
Honoré de Balzac	*Colonel Chabert*	A.N. Wilson
Charles Baudelaire	*On Wine and Hashish*	Margaret Drabble
Aphra Behn	*The Lover's Watch*	
Giovanni Boccaccio	*Life of Dante*	A.N. Wilson
Charlotte Brontë	*The Foundling*	
Charlotte Brontë	*The Green Dwarf*	Libby Purves
Charlotte Brontë	*The Secret*	Salley Vickers
Charlotte Brontë	*The Spell*	Nicola Barker
Emily Brontë	*Poems of Solitude*	Helen Dunmore
Giacomo Casanova	*The Duel*	Tim Parks
Miguel de Cervantes	*The Dialogue of the Dogs*	Ben Okri
Geoffrey Chaucer	*The Parliament of Birds*	
Anton Chekhov	*The Story of a Nobody*	Louis de Bernières
Anton Chekhov	*Three Years*	William Fiennes
Wilkie Collins	*The Frozen Deep*	
Wilkie Collins	*A Rogue's Life*	Peter Ackroyd

Ugo Foscolo	*Last Letters of Jacopo Ortis*	Valerio Massimo Manfredi
Giuseppe Garibaldi	*My Life*	Tim Parks
Elizabeth Gaskell	*Lois the Witch*	Jenny Uglow
Theophile Gautier	*The Jinx*	Gilbert Adair
André Gide	*Theseus*	
Johann Wolfgang von Goethe	*The Man of Fifty*	A.S. Byatt
Nikolai Gogol	*The Squabble*	Patrick McCabe
Thomas Hardy	*Fellow-Townsmen*	Emma Tennant
L.P. Hartley	*Simonetta Perkins*	Margaret Drabble
Nathaniel Hawthorne	*Rappaccini's Daughter*	Simon Schama
E.T.A. Hoffmann	*Mademoiselle de Scudéri*	Gilbert Adair
Victor Hugo	*The Last Day of a Condemned Man*	Libby Purves
Joris-Karl Huysmans	*With the Flow*	Simon Callow
Henry James	*In the Cage*	Libby Purves
John Keats	*Fugitive Poems*	Andrew Motion
D.H. Lawrence	*Daughters of the Vicar*	Anita Desai
D.H. Lawrence	*The Fox*	Doris Lessing
Giacomo Leopardi	*Thoughts*	Edoardo Albinati
Mikhail Lermontov	*A Hero of Our Time*	Doris Lessing
Nikolai Leskov	*Lady Macbeth of Mtsensk*	Gilbert Adair
Jack London	*Before Adam*	
Niccolò Machiavelli	*Life of Castruccio Castracani*	Richard Overy
Xavier de Maistre	*A Journey Around my Room*	Alain de Botton
Edgar Lee Masters	*Spoon River Anthology*	Shena Mackay
Guy de Maupassant	*Butterball*	Germaine Greer
Lorenzino de' Medici	*Apology for a Murder*	Tim Parks
Herman Melville	*The Enchanted Isles*	Margaret Drabble
Prosper Mérimée	*Carmen*	Philip Pullman